Avery drove as fast as possible toward Dallas's cabin.

She had no idea if the ̲̲̲̲̲̲̲̲̲̲̲̲̲̲̲̲̲̲̲̲̲ that had attacked her, ̲̲̲̲̲̲̲̲̲̲̲̲̲̲̲̲̲̲̲̲̲ after her or not. She gr̲̲̲̲̲̲̲̲̲̲̲̲̲̲̲̲̲̲̲ of her purse but was to̲̲̲̲̲̲̲̲̲̲̲̲̲̲̲̲̲̲̲̲ make a call.

Fear still clawed at her throat as her eyes shot to her rearview mirror over and over again. She didn't see anyone following her yet, but she feared the truck would suddenly appear right behind her once again.

She finally pulled up in front of Dallas's cabin and pulled to a halt next to his truck. Safety. She continued to sob as she took her phone and raced for his front door.

"Dallas!" She beat on the door with her fist. Fear was still a frantic, screaming beast inside her. There was no answer. She banged on the door once again. "Dallas, please help me!"

* * *

If you're on Twitter, tell us what you think of Harlequin Romantic Suspense! #harlequinromsuspense

Dear Reader,

We love our Coltons, and what could be better than a Colton book that includes a serial killer and a surprise pregnancy?

It was such fun writing Avery Logan and Dallas Colton's story. I love to write about people exploring the possibility of love. It makes me remember falling in love with my husband.

Of course, for Avery and Dallas, all is not smooth. There are definitely bumps in the road for these two...bumps and danger. If you want to know if they survive and if true love manages to overcome the darkness that is thrown in their paths, then you just need to read the book!

As always, happy reading!

Carla Cassidy

COLTON 911: TARGET IN JEOPARDY

Carla Cassidy

HARLEQUIN® ROMANTIC SUSPENSE

Special thanks and acknowledgment are given to Carla Cassidy for her contribution to the Colton 911 miniseries.

ISBN-13: 978-1-335-66214-9

Colton 911: Target in Jeopardy

Copyright © 2019 by Harlequin Books S.A.

Recycling programs for this product may not exist in your area.

Printed in U.S.A.

Carla Cassidy is an award-winning, *New York Times* bestselling author who has written more than 120 novels for Harlequin. In 1995, she won Best Silhouette Romance from *RT Book Reviews* for *Anything for Danny*. In 1998, she won a Career Achievement Award for Best Innovative Series from *RT Book Reviews*. Carla believes the only thing better than curling up with a good book to read is sitting down at the computer with a good story to write.

Books by Carla Cassidy

Harlequin Romantic Suspense

Colton 911

Colton 911: Target in Jeopardy

Cowboys of Holiday Ranch

A Real Cowboy
Cowboy of Interest
Cowboy Under Fire
Cowboy at Arms
Operation Cowboy Daddy
Killer Cowboy
Sheltered by the Cowboy
Guardian Cowboy
Cowboy Defender

The Coltons of Red Ridge

The Colton Cowboy

The Coltons of Shadow Creek

Colton's Secret Son

Visit the Author Profile page at Harlequin.com for more titles.

Chapter 1

Avery Logan slowly walked up the stairs to the courthouse's front door. She paused for a moment before going inside the stately three-story brick building where justice was handed out on a daily basis.

She took her job very seriously. She always arrived early and took a moment or two to relax on the top concrete step before heading inside to face her job as a criminal prosecutor.

There were several other people standing around and waiting for the courthouse to officially open its doors to the public, including some who would find out their fate.

She shifted her briefcase from one hand to the other and drew in a deep breath of the September air. Autumn was her favorite time of the year. The changing colors of the trees in Whisperwood, Texas, were particularly pretty this year. Deep reds battled with shades of orange and yellow, and created a vision of nature at its finest.

Optimism buoyed her in spite of the fact that her feet already hurt and her lower back ached. Today was the last of the witnesses, and hopefully final arguments would occur by noon. She was relatively sure as prosecutor that this was going to be a win for Lady Justice. Although Dwayne Conway wasn't the big drug lord she dreamed of bringing down, if she'd done her job right at least he'd be one more lowlife drug-selling creep off the streets.

A sharp, stabbing pain shot through her. Her heart suddenly wept a single name… Zeke. Since his death a little over a year ago, a day didn't go by that she didn't grieve for him. He'd been her best friend and her beloved younger brother, and a heroin overdose had taken him away from her forever.

She shoved thoughts of Zeke away and took one more glance around at the people gathered at the foot of the stairs. Suddenly she froze.

He stood with a small group, including Forrest Colton, who was due to testify in the trial today. Was it really him or was she just imagining it?

"Dallas." His name whispered from her lips as a thousand emotions rushed over her. She stared at the man's profile, drinking in the sight of his wavy, sandy-colored hair and his straight nose. Yes, there was no question in her mind, it was him. She knew his eyes were an azure blue and that he had an utterly charming smile.

She also knew what it felt like to be held in his strong arms and how his sexy lips could kiss a woman completely mindless. She knew what it felt like to make exquisite love with him. What she didn't know was his last name.

She wrapped an arm around her burgeoning stomach, and at the same time he turned and looked up. His eyes widened in obvious stunned surprise at the sight of her. His gaze swept the length of her body, pausing on the huge baby bump that had annihilated her waistline months ago, and then his gaze trekked back up to her face.

She remained frozen in place, not sure what to do. Should she turn around and run? What was his reaction going to be? It wasn't like she really knew him. They'd shared only a single night together, a passionate night fueled by a little too much alcohol and loneliness. It had also been a foolish night without birth control or protection.

He said something to the others in the group and then slowly climbed the stairs to where she stood. Her heart beat a million miles a minute as he drew closer.

He was just as handsome as she remembered, with

his light hair, intense blue eyes and well-defined features. She held her breath as he finally reached her.

"Avery," he said in greeting.

"Hi, Dallas. It's been a while." Good Lord, this was definitely the most awkward moment she'd ever experienced in all of her thirty-three years. His gaze once again lingered on her very pregnant belly. "Uh…yes," she said, answering what she knew his question might be.

He shifted from one foot to the other, as if at a loss for words, and his face instantly paled. She had only a couple minutes left before she needed to be in her seat in the courtroom. "Uh, it's nice to see you again," she said. "I need to get inside." She turned toward the door, but he stopped her.

"Avery, obviously we need to talk." He pulled his wallet out of his black slacks' pocket and drew out a business card and handed it to her. "That's got all my contact information on it. Could we maybe meet somewhere later today, after you're finished here?"

"I'm hoping this case goes to the jury around noon. I could meet you at JoJo's Java after that."

"That would be good," he replied soberly.

"I really need to get inside now." This time when she turned toward the door he didn't stop her.

It wasn't until she went through security and walked toward the courtroom where the trial was taking place that she finally drew a deep, unsteady breath.

What a shock, to suddenly see the man who had been only a memory in her thoughts for the past seven and a half months. He had looked as handsome as he had on the night she'd first met him. His slacks had fit perfectly on his slim hips and long legs. The gray dress shirt he wore had loved his lean muscles and broad shoulders.

Now that he knew she was pregnant what would happen? Would he really believe he was the father? She'd certainly fallen into bed with him easily enough; would he believe she did that with other men, as well? He was the one and only man she'd been with for a very long time. If he wanted a DNA test, she would understand and she would gladly comply.

She was pleased that he knew. As the father he had a right to know. If she'd known how to contact him she would have done so when she had first found out she was pregnant.

Would he want to be a part of this? Would he want to be an involved father? Or would he disappear once again and have nothing to do with her? As far as she was concerned he didn't owe her anything. She'd been foolish enough to have sex without protection and it had been her choice to have the babies.

She looked at the card he had handed her. Dallas Colton. His last name was Colton. That name was certainly a familiar one in Whisperwood, Texas. The Cowboy Heroes were a horseback rescue team that ventured into disaster zones and rescued the stranded, and several of the Colton men were a part of it. They were both EMTs and ranchers, and all of them were specialists in search and rescue.

Most recently they had been instrumental in saving lives when Hurricane Brooke had roared through the small town, leaving behind destruction from high winds, flooding waters and the horrific tornadoes that had been spawned by the storm.

She reached the courtroom and took her place on the prosecutor's side of the room. She opened her briefcase and tucked the business card inside one of the pockets, and then withdrew the papers she would need for the day.

As the courtroom began to fill, she tried to get her mind off Dallas. She had to focus on the task at hand, prosecuting a dope dealer, but her mind continued to fill with memories of the night she had shared with Dallas.

She'd gone to Bailey's Bar with her best friend, PI Summer Davies, with the intention of drinking her stress and sorrow away. She had still been deeply grieving her brother's death and she'd been working on a case that had included her receiving death threats.

She'd already had a couple drinks when he'd walked in. He'd been one hot piece of eye candy clad in his army uniform, and when their gazes had met a sweet heat had rushed through her. Eventually

Summer had left the bar, but Avery had stayed and the handsome army sergeant had approached her.

He'd told her he was on leave and in town visiting relatives. She didn't ask who the relatives were, and he didn't offer any names. Instead they had shared more drinks and talked about nothing too important.

The sexual energy between them had been off the charts and that night she had done something she'd never done before. They had left the bar and gone to the nearby motel, and there she'd had a one-night stand.

She'd awakened the next morning with a desire to get to know him better, to build on their incredible physical attraction. However, he'd told her in no uncertain terms that he wanted nothing more from her. She'd left the motel and had never seen or heard from him again, until now.

Forrest Colton was a witness in the trial and that meant Dallas was probably going to sit in the courtroom. She couldn't turn around. She didn't want to see him right now when she had such an important job to do. But it was a bit disquieting to realize he'd be watching her.

"All rise." The bailiff's deep, loud voice yanked her from her thoughts. It was definitely time for her to focus on her job. Dwayne Conway was a punk, a thug who had sold pain pills and a rock of cocaine to an undercover cop. Forrest Colton had witnessed the illegal transaction and would be called to the stand to corroborate the cop's story.

Dwayne was low-hanging fruit of a rotten tree that grew in Whisperwood, a tree of drugs and corruption that was getting bigger and bigger every day. Avery was on the front line of the fight to get all drugs, especially the deadly heroin, off the streets of the town she loved.

Just as she had figured, it was eleven thirty when she made her closing arguments, and by noon the case was given to the jury.

She and the defense attorney met with the judge for a few last-minute paperwork details and then she was free until the jury returned with a verdict. Hopefully, that would happen fairly quickly and another bottom-feeder would be off the streets.

There was no sign of Dallas when she left the courtroom. She assumed he knew she would be heading to JoJo's Java to meet with him.

As she headed toward her car in the parking lot behind the building, butterflies danced in her stomach. She'd scarcely had time to process the fact that Dallas was here, let alone that she was going to meet with him in just a few minutes.

The butterflies grew more active as she pulled out of the parking lot and onto the main drag. She'd fantasized about this moment for the entire seven and a half months of her pregnancy.

There had been no question in her mind that Dallas was the father. Before that night with him it had been over a year since she'd had sex, and that with a man she'd dated for only three months.

There had been few men in her life. Before Zeke's death she'd been too career oriented to want any long-term relationships, and since Zeke's death that was the last thing she wanted.

She parked in a space in front of the trendy coffee shop. For a moment she remained seated in the car and gently caressed her stomach, wondering how reality would stack up to fantasy.

With a small sigh, she got out of her car and headed inside to find out what would happen now that Dallas was here.

Dallas Colton sat at a table for two toward the back of JoJo's Java, with a cup of black coffee before him. The coffee shop was a popular place for people to gather in town. Along with the tables and chairs, there was a long bar and an outdoor patio. Amber lighting overhead provided a warm, cozy feeling.

He wasn't feeling all warm and cozy right now. He was still very much reeling from seeing Avery again…a very pregnant Avery.

When he'd first looked up and seen her standing on the top step of the courthouse, his heart had crashed against his ribs. Not that his heart had been involved with her at all, but he'd been momentarily stunned by her beauty.

Her long, reddish-brown hair had sparkled in the sunlight and he suddenly remembered that her eyes were the green of a dark, mysterious forest.

When he'd seen her pregnant stomach, he'd known instinctively that the baby was his. Birth control and protection had been the last things on his mind when he'd left the bar with her and gone to the nearby motel almost eight months before.

It had been a night of crazy, wild passion. That night he'd wrapped his arms around Avery in an effort to momentarily staunch his grief over another woman.

Ivy. Her name whispered through him, along with a swell of all-too-familiar anguish. Oh God, he couldn't think about her right now. It felt like such a betrayal to think about her while he met with a woman who was probably carrying his baby. He consciously willed those thoughts away and took a drink of his coffee.

Right now his complete focus needed to be on Avery and the very real possibility that the baby she carried was his. The timing was certainly right for that to be. If that was the case, he needed to figure out what came next.

Was she in a relationship with another man? Was it possible she had married since he had been with her? He frowned. He wasn't sure he liked the idea of another man raising his child.

Maybe he was jumping way ahead of himself.

Maybe the baby she carried wasn't his. But she'd indicated it was and his gut told him it was his.

Jeez. A baby. This was certainly not the way he'd envisioned himself becoming a father…a one-night stand with a woman he didn't really know.

He wouldn't have even been at the courthouse this morning if his brother hadn't been testifying. At the last minute Dallas had decided to go along and offer Forrest his support.

He looked toward the entrance at the same time Avery came through the door. She looked around and then spotted him. She held up a hand and pointed toward the counter, then walked over to it and placed an order. Despite her condition, she walked with a confidence that was both powerful and yet graceful. He found it very attractive.

He'd been entranced as she'd given her closing arguments minutes earlier. She'd been so impassioned, demanding rather than pleading for votes of guilt. She was obviously very smart and articulate, and yet had connected with the jury on an emotional level.

Her black slacks emphasized her slender legs. Her red blouse elegantly skimmed the fullness of her belly. In spite of her current condition, the memory of their night together was suddenly a hot burn in his brain. It had been a night of intense pleasure. She'd been a giving lover and the experience of having sex with her was emblazoned in his mind.

As she paid for a cup of something, he tried to

shove those provocative memories out of his head. This whole thing felt so surreal and so very awkward.

She eased down in the chair opposite his and brought with her a scent of an exotic spice and citrus fragrance that he instantly remembered from their night together.

He tightened his fingers around his warm, plastic-foam cup and worked up a smile that hopefully didn't show how very ill at ease he was under the circumstances.

"There's nothing better to calm the nerves than a hot cup of herbal tea," she said, to break the ice.

Maybe he should have opted for some of that tea instead of the coffee that now sat heavy in his chest. He had so many questions, yet at the moment, sitting across from her, he was uncharacteristically tongue-tied. "Why didn't you tell me?" The words finally blurted out of him.

She raised an eyebrow. "How could I have told you? I only knew your first name and that you were in the army. I had no idea where you were stationed or how to contact you. We didn't exactly exchange phone numbers and addresses that night."

Her cheeks flushed with a pretty pink color. "You can believe it or not, but that was the first and only time I've ever done something like that in my entire life. It was a night of risky behavior and that isn't who I am. You were the only man I'd been with for a very long time."

He really had no reason to believe her, but he did. Despite their wild desire that night, there had also been a shyness, an awkwardness about her that had let him know it wasn't something she did all the time.

She didn't need to know he'd acted out of character that night, as well. Driven into the bar with a deep grief, he'd intended to drink himself into oblivion. Although he'd had more than his share of booze that night, it had been Avery's smile that had prompted him to try to lose his grief in her rather than the bottom of a bottle.

It hadn't worked. He'd awakened the next morning hungover and with his grief still intact, and a new guilt weighing heavy in his heart. The only real difference had been he'd had a beautiful woman in his arms who had wanted more from him than he could give.

"I would have loved to contact you when I first found out I was pregnant, but I couldn't. I had no idea how to find you." Her hand dropped to her stomach. "I don't expect anything from you, Dallas. I made the decision to have these babies and I'm fine doing this all on my own."

A shocked surprise jolted through him. "B-b-babies?" he stuttered.

She nodded and smiled. "I'm carrying twins...a boy and a girl."

He couldn't help the small gasp that escaped him. He hadn't even completely processed that she was pregnant with one baby, let alone two.

She frowned and stared down into her cup for a long moment and then glanced back at him. "Look, I know this has to be a big shock to you," she said. "I really don't need anything from you, Dallas. I'll be fine on my own."

"You aren't getting rid of me that easily," he immediately replied. This might not be the time or the way he would have chosen to become a father, but that didn't matter. Now he knew she carried his son and his daughter and he wasn't about to walk away from his babies.

"Uh...do you have a significant other in your life right now?" he asked.

She laughed, the sound rich and melodic. "Right, I've had to beat the men away from me and my girlish figure." She sobered and then sighed. "Sorry, I didn't mean to be sarcastic, and no, there's no significant other in my life. I've never even wanted one. I've been pretty focused on my career. What about you?"

"No, there's nobody," he replied. Unless he counted the ghost of a woman who haunted him, a ghost he just couldn't let go of because the pain of loss, of utter emptiness, would be too great for him to endure.

"When do you leave to go back to where you're stationed?" she asked.

"I don't. I'm now former Army Sergeant Dallas

Colton. I finalized my discharge three months ago and I'm here in Whisperwood to stay."

"Oh, I'm surprised we haven't run into each other before now," she replied.

"I'm living in an old foreman's cabin out on the ranch, and for the last couple of months I've been doing what I can to help with the cleanup after the hurricane. I don't get into town much." His gaze once again took in the sight of her stomach. "Should you still be working?"

"Actually, this was my last case. Once the jury comes back I am officially on maternity leave. It's time for me to nest."

"Nest?"

She smiled. She had a beautiful smile that lit up her features and warmed whoever it was directed at. It had been her smile that had initially grabbed his attention in the bar that night, and that warmth now swept over him.

"You know, I'll make sure I have everything ready for the babies when they arrive. I'll get a manicure and a pedicure and make sure I get extra sleep and relax before they get here."

"Do you have everything you need for when they do get here?" he asked.

"Yes. My coworkers gave me a big baby shower last month and they were all very generous. I told you I didn't need anything from you, Dallas, and I meant it. There's only one person here in town who knows you are the father and that's my closest friend. She would never tell anyone. I would love for you to be a part of their lives. I certainly believe it's important for children to have both parents involved, but I understand if you just want to walk away."

"What would make you think I'm the kind of man who would just walk away from this?"

She tilted her head and gazed at him intently. "Dallas, I really don't know what kind of a man you are."

And he didn't know what kind of woman she was. Oh, he knew how hot her kisses were and how her bare skin felt against his. He knew how her sweet moans had sounded against the side of his neck. But, that was really all he knew about her.

"I think it would be nice if we got to know each other better," he said. Actually, he thought it was a necessity in this crazy circumstance.

"And how do we do that?" she asked.

"Why don't we start with me taking you out to dinner at the Bluebell Diner tomorrow night?" he replied.

She looked at him in surprise. "Uh…okay, that would be nice." Her cell phone rang. "Excuse me," she murmured, and took the call. It lasted only a minute and then she hung up and gathered her purse and briefcase.

"I'm sorry. The jury has returned and I've got to get back to the courthouse."

He stood as she did. "That was fast."

She flashed him that beautiful smile again. "And hopefully a good sign."

"Shall we say six tomorrow evening?" he asked.

"That sounds perfect. I'll text you my address and I'll see you then."

He watched as she headed toward the door and then he sank back down into his chair. Twins. Jeez, this was the very last thing he'd expected when he'd driven into town this morning to be a support to his brother. Heck, in a million years he couldn't have expected to suddenly discover he was about to become the father of twins.

He took a sip of his now cold coffee and leaned back in the chair. Two babies. A little boy and a little girl. He was going to be a father, and fairly quickly. With the initial shock slowly wearing off came a sense of anticipation...a sense of unexpected joy.

He hadn't expected to ever feel that again, not after losing his wife. When he'd buried Ivy, he'd believed he'd also buried his heart and soul with her. Any hope for future happiness, for joy or laughter, had gone into that grave with her.

But this...this sudden surprise, this miracle of two little souls who would be forever connected to him brought with it a glimmer of hope. They were a promise of a happiness he'd never dreamed of and had never thought possible before.

He had no idea if he even liked Avery. There was

a possibility that once they spent a little time together she might not like him.

But like it or not, somehow, some way they needed to figure things out, because for the next eighteen years or so they would be in each other's lives due to their mutual love of a baby boy and a baby girl.

Chapter 2

With a groan, Avery pulled the black-and-white-checkered maternity blouse over her head and threw it on the bed to join the others she'd tried on and then rejected.

Clad in just her black maternity slacks and a bra, she went back to her closet to make yet another selection. She knew she was being utterly ridiculous. It was just dinner at the Bluebell Diner. Any one of the blouses on the bed would have been just fine to wear for the meal out.

Still, she was ridiculously nervous and determined to look her very best. It wasn't just a meal out, it was the first time she would spend real time with a man who would be in her life in one way or another for a very long time to come. Unless he chose not to be.

"Somehow, some way, everything is going to be okay, right, Lulu?"

The black toy poodle sitting in the doorway of her room barked happily at the sound of her name. At the same time the babies kicked, and it felt as if they turned somersaults in her belly. She had yet to pick out names for them, which was probably a good thing, since now Dallas might want to be a part of that process.

Aware of time ticking by, she focused on the clothes in her closet once again. Her gaze landed on a pink-and-black-striped blouse. The last time she'd worn it she had gotten several compliments. She yanked it from the hanger and then pulled it on over her head. She closed her closet door to insure she wouldn't change her mind yet again.

As she went into the adjoining bathroom to put on her makeup, she fought against a new flurry of nerves. Despite the fact that she and Dallas had been intimate with each other, he was a virtual stranger to her.

What if they really didn't like each other? What if their views of life were completely different? What if they clashed in every area that was important? After having time to digest the news of her pregnancy, would he resent her for getting pregnant? Would he feel like she was somehow trying to trap him?

It wasn't like she was asking him to marry her. In fact, that was the very last thing she wanted. Losing Zeke had changed her, made her reluctant to ever care deeply about anyone ever again. She had no desire for a partner or to be married, but these babies were part of her, they were her family, and she would shower them with all the love she had in her heart.

She tried to tamp down the concerns about Dallas as she applied her eye makeup and then added pink-tinted gloss to her lips. She ran her brush through her hair and then spritzed on perfume and called herself ready.

She left the bathroom and went into the living room and sat on the edge of the sofa. He should be arriving within the next fifteen minutes or so. Lulu sat at her feet, gazing up at her adoringly.

She picked up the dog and then looked around, assured by the neat-and-tidy condition of her living room. She'd spent the morning cleaning, to make sure the house was in tip-top shape just in case Dallas came in.

She'd bought the three-bedroom ranch house right after she'd learned she was pregnant. She hadn't wanted her babies to be raised in the small apartment where she'd been living at the time, and in any case, she had been thinking about purchasing a house.

The minute she'd seen this place she'd known it was a perfect fit. Not only did it have the three bedrooms and a big eat-in kitchen, but it also had a large fenced-in backyard that would be perfect for growing children.

Every move she had made, every decision she'd reached in the last seven months had been in what she believed was the best interest of her little family.

Family. She felt as if she'd lost every member of her family, and having these babies had been her chance to create a new family unit for herself.

It was impossible to think about family without thinking about Zeke, and thoughts of him always brought a sharp grief that even after a year still had the ability to almost take her breath away.

If only she had done something differently. If only she had—

The ring of her cell phone pulled her from her thoughts. She set Lulu on the floor and dug in her purse for the phone. She looked at the caller identification and then answered. "Hi, Chad."

"How's our pregnant lady?" Chad Ruland asked.

Avery smiled at the sound of her fellow prosecutor's deep voice. "The pregnant lady is doing just fine."

"I've got Danny here with me and he'd like to talk to you." Danny Jenkins was a file clerk, and he and Chad had been wonderfully supportive throughout her pregnancy.

A knock sounded at her door. "Chad, I've got to go. Tell Danny I'll call him later." She rose from the sofa as nerves fluttered wildly inside her. She and Chad said their goodbyes.

"You be good while I'm gone," she said to Lulu. She grabbed her purse and then opened the door. "Hi," she said.

Jeez, Dallas looked so darned hot in a pair of black jeans and a long-sleeved black polo shirt that emphasized his broad shoulders and flat abdomen. He looked like a cowboy in a pinup calendar, and she looked like a pink-and-black-striped beached whale.

"Hi," he replied. "Are you all ready to go?"

Lulu gave a cheerful bark, her tail wagging in anticipation of meeting a new friend, but Avery quickly stepped out of the house and then closed her door behind her and made sure it was locked.

"Sounds like you have a friend in there," he said.

"I do. A friendly little poodle named Lulu. She's two years old and a complete sweetheart. It's a nice evening," she said, changing the subject as they walked toward his truck, parked in her driveway. The air was just a bit crisp, cooler than usual for early September.

"It is," he agreed. "Fall seems to be arriving a bit ahead of time this year."

"That's okay with me. Out of all of the seasons, fall is my favorite."

"I like it, too. Are you hungry?"

She laughed. "I'm always hungry. Eating for three is a responsibility I take very seriously."

"Well then, let's get the three of you fed as soon as

possible," he replied with an easy smile. He opened the passenger door for her and then helped her inside.

His smile had gone a long way in easing some of her nerves. This dinner wasn't supposed to do anything but allow them to get to know each other better. It was a first date without the expectation of any romance.

Even knowing that, she couldn't help the way her heart beat just a little bit faster in his presence. Hormones, she told herself...crazy, pregnant hormones. That had to be why a pleasant energy raced through her as he got into the truck, bringing with him a scent of minty soap and a clean, fresh-scented cologne.

"It looks like this is a nice neighborhood," he said, as he backed out of her driveway.

"It is nice. I bought the place soon after I found out I was pregnant, so picking a good neighborhood and a nice house was very important to me."

"I'm sorry you've had to go through so much of this process alone. Do you have family here?"

Her heart constricted. "I have my father, but we aren't really close."

"I'm sorry to hear that."

"Thanks, but it is what it is."

"By the way, congratulations. I heard through the grapevine you got your man yesterday." He shot her a quick glance. "I'm not surprised. You were quite passionate in your closing argument."

She smiled. "I'm quite passionate about getting bad guys behind bars, especially drug dealers."

By that time they had arrived at the restaurant. The Bluebell Diner was located on Main Street, along with the general store, Lone Star Pharma, a corner store and Kain's Garage. There were also various other kinds of businesses on the main drag, like a grocery store and an ice cream parlor.

Since it was Friday, the parking spaces in front of the diner were all full. It was definitely a popular place for the people in Whisperwood to dine, especially on the weekends.

"Why don't I drop you off here at the door and I'll find a parking space down the block," he suggested.

"Oh no, that isn't necessary," she protested. "Walking is actually good for me."

"If you're sure…"

"It's fine," she assured him. "I could use the exercise."

He found an empty space in the next block and they got out of the truck to walk back to the diner. As they went they chatted about the storefronts they passed. She pointed out the boutique where she had bought most of her maternity clothes, and he told her where he bought his cowboy boots. They both agreed that Edwards's Ice Cream Parlor was a favorite place to visit.

Within minutes they entered the busy diner. The air inside smelled of simmering meats and baked goods, of rich sauces and vegetables. Avery's appetite came to life. The sounds of people talking and laughing and the clinking of glass and silverware filled the room.

They wove their way to the back and quickly staked claim to a blue-and-white-gingham-tablecloth-clad booth. "At least the noise level is a little less intense back here," he said, once they were settled in.

"You do realize you're going to be the object of gossip after this evening," she said. She'd been acutely aware of the curious stares that had followed them from the diner's front door to their booth.

"Gossip has never scared me," he replied easily, and then frowned. "Does it bother you?"

"Heavens, no. I've been the subject of town gossip since the moment my pregnancy started to show and there was no man in my life," she replied.

"Then I have a feeling the two of us are going to generate a lot more gossip in the future," he said drily.

"I'm happy to keep the busybodies busy."

He grinned at her. "I like the way you think." His grin was a wide, warm one that shot an unexpected heat through her.

Thankfully, at that moment Susan Blake, one of the waitresses, appeared at their booth. She greeted them and handed them each a menu. "How are you folks this evening?" she asked pleasantly.

"We're good," Avery replied.

"What can I get you both to drink?" Susan asked.

"Water is fine for me," Avery said.

"I'll take a cup of coffee," Dallas added.

"I'll be right back with those drinks and to take your food orders." With that, Susan left their booth.

Avery opened the menu and Dallas did the same. She was acutely aware of the man across from her even as she studied the food offerings.

His energy wafted across the table to her. He seemed to command the space around him. He had a quiet confidence about himself that was vastly appealing to her.

But did that confidence manifest itself in arrogance? Was he a control freak? Was it his way or the highway? So far there had been no indication that he was any of those things, but time would tell, and it was important for her to learn exactly what kind of a man he was and what kind of a father he would be.

"What looks good to you?" His gaze held hers over the top of the menus. His eyes were like crystal blue waters, waters she had easily drowned in seven and a half months ago, but certainly wouldn't be drowning in again.

"Everything looks good to me," she replied with a small laugh. "Actually, I think I'm going to go with the chicken-fried steak and mashed potatoes. The kids seem to crave comfort food lately."

"Have you had any strange cravings like I've heard pregnant women do?" he asked.

"Green olives with potato chips," she confessed. "I never really liked green olives before I got pregnant, but now when I snack I want olives and salt-and-vinegar potato chips."

"An interesting combination," he replied.

"Some people might say it's a gross combination," she said ruefully. She was rewarded by his laughter. It was a wonderful sound, deep and rich, and she immediately wanted to hear it again. "So, what are you ordering?" she asked him.

He closed the menu. "I'm having the meat loaf special. I'm pretty fond of comfort food, too."

Susan returned to their table with their drinks and then took their food orders and disappeared once again. Dallas stared down into his coffee cup for a moment and then gazed at Avery.

"When you found out you were pregnant did you, uh, consider other options?"

"No," she replied firmly. "I never considered anything other than having the babies. I was at a place in my life where I wanted to start my family, but not only did I not have a significant other in my life, I didn't really want a significant other. These babies felt like a gift from heaven to me and I never considered anything but giving them life."

"I feel like they're a gift from heaven, too. Uh… did you have morning sickness?" He looked slightly uncomfortable and this time his smile was sheepish.

"I don't mean to pry. I just feel like I've missed out on so much."

"Dallas, I don't feel like your prying, and please feel free to ask me whatever you want to know. I'm an open book." Actually, she was glad that he wanted to know what he'd missed so far about her pregnancy.

Maybe that meant he really was planning on sticking around and being in the babies' lives. "I was one of the lucky ones who didn't have much morning sickness. I have had some heartburn, but nothing really severe."

She didn't want to share with him the moments of intense loneliness she'd suffered during the last seven and a half months, a loneliness that had surprised her.

It had to be because she didn't have Zeke in her life anymore. Zeke, who would have made an awesome uncle. She didn't want Dallas to know that there had been lots of times she'd desperately wished somebody special was around to share the wonder of pregnancy with her.

There had also been moments when she'd felt bad that her babies would not have a father in their lives. She had been acutely aware that it was a choice she had made for them and not a choice they would have made for themselves.

"That's good. Overall, how are you feeling?"

"Totally fat." She laughed. "I know it's all baby fat, but it's starting to get difficult to get comfortable and by the end of the day I usually have a back-ache. But it won't be long and they'll be here, and I know the minute I hold them in my arms I'll forget any aches and pains I've had."

Once again his gaze held hers intently. "I just want you to know that from here on out, you aren't alone in this. From here on out, Avery, I intend to be by your side. And you don't look fat, you look pregnant and pretty."

"Thank you," she replied, as the warmth of a blush filled her cheeks.

His words found that empty well of loneliness inside her and filled it up. They also brought unexpected tears to burn her eyes. She'd thought she was fine and strong to have the babies by herself, and she would have been. But it was nice that he was here now, nice that she didn't have to go through the rest of this all alone, and that there was a real possibility her babies would have their father in their lives.

Thankfully, at that moment Susan arrived to deliver their dinner, and Avery managed to get her crazy emotions under control.

The main thing she had to remember was the handsome, seemingly kind and slightly shy man across from her was only with her for one reason… because she was pregnant with his babies.

He cared about her only because she was carrying his children. She had to remember he wasn't with her because he had any kind of a romantic interest in her.

* * *

As they ate their meal the conversation stayed light and easy, even though there were a hundred things Dallas wanted to know about Avery.

He told himself he had to be patient. He didn't want her to feel like he was coming at her with all his questions at once. He certainly didn't want to force anything. He just wanted this new and unusual relationship to grow naturally.

It would be great if they could become good friends for the sake of the babies. In truth, he felt like that was vital. They would be sharing custody, and as the twins grew older it would be imperative that he and Avery be a united front in terms of discipline and everything else.

He smiled inwardly at his own thoughts. The babies weren't even born yet and he already had them as teenagers who might need parental control.

One thing was for certain. She'd said she looked fat, but that wasn't true. She made a beautiful pregnant woman. Yes, her belly was big and round, but that was the only place she looked like she'd gained weight.

Her skin looked warm and so…so touchable, and she also appeared to glow from within. The black-and-pink-ink blouse made the green of her eyes appear clear and bright. But her beauty had nothing to do with the relationship they needed to build.

"Tell me more about your job," he now said. "How long have you been a prosecutor?"

"Only for the past year," she replied. "Before that I was a defense attorney."

"What made you change?" he asked curiously.

Her green eyes darkened with shadows just before she gazed down at her plate. She took a moment and then looked back at him. "Whether anyone wants to acknowledge it or not, there's a growing drug problem in this town."

She paused and then continued, her eyes showing a blaze of passion that vanquished the shadows. "Everyone says drug abuse is a victimless crime, but that's so not true. I've seen the devastation left behind in families when somebody overdoses and dies. I've seen families torn apart by a drug addict who is stealing from them and lying to them to support a habit. My mission now is to see that when the police arrest drug dealers, they stay behind bars."

"A noble mission," he replied. What he didn't say was that there was a lot more going on in Whisperwood than drug sales. There was no reason to include murder and a serial killer in their conversation, and potentially change the positive vibe they had between them right now.

Still, she looked wonderfully attractive with that blaze in her eyes and her cheeks flushed with her emotion. She'd looked that way when they had made love. He glanced down into his coffee cup and shoved the inappropriate thoughts out of his head.

As they finished the meal they each talked more about their jobs. She told him about some of the more colorful and funny things that had happened in her work in court.

In turn he told her about some of the rescues he'd been a part of after the hurricane's floodwaters had swept through the vicinity. "We're still doing cleanup in several areas."

By that time they had finished with their dinner. "Are you up for dessert?" he asked.

"Oh no, I'm too full of mashed potatoes and gravy to even think about dessert," she protested. "But you feel free to order some."

"No, I'm good to go." He signaled to Susan for their tab.

"I'm happy to go dutch," she said.

"That's unnecessary," he replied.

"Dallas, I'm used to paying my own way."

He smiled at her. "For tonight please allow this army sergeant turned cowboy to buy your dinner."

"Okay, and thank you. But if we go out to eat again, then you must let me pay my own way."

"I see a lot of meals out in our future," he replied.

"Or maybe I could cook for you," she replied.

"Are you a good cook?"

"I think I am. I don't do anything too fancy, but I can put a pretty decent meal on the table."

At that time Susan returned to the table with their tab. Dallas paid cash, left a tip and then he and Avery got up from the booth.

She walked ahead of him past the other booths still filled with diners. She had reached the last one when a young man suddenly got up and slammed into her side, nearly knocking her into a nearby table.

"Hey," Dallas said. He grabbed Avery to him, grateful that she hadn't fallen.

"Sorry," the man muttered. "I didn't see her." He stared at Avery for a long moment and then slid back into his booth as one of the young men with him snickered.

"It's okay," Avery said, and moved out of his embrace. Dallas followed her to exit the diner.

"Are you sure you're all right?" he asked with concern as they walked toward his truck.

"I'm fine," she replied.

"What a creep," he said. "He could have seriously hurt you." He thought of that moment when the man had held Avery's gaze. "Do you know him?"

"Unfortunately, I do. His name is Joel Asman, and he runs in the same crowd as Dwayne Conway."

"The man you put behind bars."

"Right."

By that time they'd reached the truck, and he helped her into the passenger seat. "So, you think he bumped into you on purpose?" he asked. The man had had punk written all over him, from his greasy dark hair to the snake tattoos that had decorated his skinny arms.

"It's possible, but really, it's no big deal," she replied.

Anyone who would push a pregnant woman was a creep in Dallas's eyes. Hell, anyone who would push a woman at all was a major creep.

Within minutes they were back at her house. He walked her to the front door, where she paused to dig keys out of her purse, and then she turned to look at him. "Would you like to come in for a cup of coffee?"

"If you're up for it then I'd love to," he replied. He wouldn't mind getting a look at the space where she lived…where his children would live.

She opened the door and immediately a little black dog was dancing at her feet, while barking doggie happiness. "I'm sorry," she said. "She loves people. She'll calm down in just a minute."

He bent down to pet the little black ball of energy. "What's her name again?"

"Lulu," she replied. "Lulu, enough. Let's go into the kitchen."

As he followed her through the living room and into the large kitchen, Lulu ran ahead of them. "Have a seat and I'll get the coffee."

He sank down in one of the chairs at the round oak table and looked around. Yellow-and-white gingham curtains hung at the large window. Yellow wooden signs with happy and optimistic sayings decorated the wall. The room felt warm and inviting.

She placed a pod in the one-serving coffeemaker on the counter and then got out a tea bag and filled a cup with water.

He continued to look around the room. A back

door held a little doggie door. "Do you have a fenced-in backyard?"

"Yes, it was one of my requirements when I was house-hunting." She placed the cup of water into the microwave and then turned to face him.

"I had three basic requirements when I started looking for houses. I wanted at least three bedrooms, an up-to-date kitchen and a fenced-in backyard. Cream or sugar?"

"No, black is fine."

As she set the cup of coffee in front of him he caught a whiff of her enticing perfume. It instantly evoked memories of the night they had spent together, a night that he now knew had had life-changing consequences.

He watched as she grabbed a doggie treat out of a drawer and gave it to Lulu. She then took her cup out of the microwave, grabbed a saucer with the tea bag on it and joined him at the table.

"From what I've seen of it, you have a very nice house," he said.

"Thank you. When you finish your coffee I'll show you the nursery."

The nursery. His heart swelled at the very thought. He still hadn't completely wrapped his head around the fact that he was going to be a father. "I'd like that," he replied.

An awkward silence ensued. She laughed suddenly, a melodious sound that made him want to join in. "I feel like I should be telling you my favorite color and what my sign is. You know, the questions most people ask when they first meet in a bar."

"We didn't ask each other those questions on the night we met," he said.

Her cheeks turned a becoming shade of pink. "As I recall, we didn't do much talking at all that night." She took a sip of her tea and then stared down into her cup.

"So, what's your sign?" he asked, breaking what might have become an awkward silence. She looked back up at him and he offered her a wide grin.

She laughed and the awkward moment between them passed. "I'm a Libra. What about you?"

"A Pisces."

She frowned. "Does that mean we're supposed to get along?"

"I have no idea. I don't know anything about the Zodiac signs, but it doesn't matter what our signs say, we are going to get along," he replied firmly. "Now, what's your favorite color?"

"Coral. And yours?"

"I've never really thought about it before, but I guess I'd say a light blue." It was another superficial conversation that didn't answer the questions he had about her, but hopefully she was feeling more comfortable with him with every minute they spent together.

She shifted in the chair and released a sigh that

sounded tired. He finished his coffee and stood. "I should go and let you get some rest."

"Before you do, let me show you the nursery." She rose from the table and gestured for him to follow her through the living room and down a hallway.

The first doorway they passed, on the right, led into a bathroom. The second room, on the left, was being used as a home office. She went into the bedroom across the hall.

The minute he stepped into the room, his heart expanded in his chest, making any conversation momentarily impossible. There were two cribs, one with pink bedding and one with blue. Both had mobiles dangling dancing bears. The curtains also had a border of dancing bears. It was a delightful and joyous room.

There was also a changing table with boxes of disposable diapers on top, and a rocking chair in one corner with two teddy bears on the cushioned seat. He realized the idea of the babies hadn't actually been real to him until this very moment.

This room was where his babies would sleep and dream. This was where their diapers and clothes would be changed. This was where they would be rocked and loved, and hopefully there would be nights when he was in that rocking chair with both his babies in his arms.

A wealth of emotion swept through him, one that made him feel both incredibly strong and achingly vulnerable at the same time.

"It's a really nice room," he finally managed to say. As he gazed at Avery he felt a closeness to her that wasn't reflective of the rather superficial relationship they'd shared so far.

He had the unexpected desire to pull her close to him, to feel her heart beating against his own. He wanted to stroke her back and make her feel cherished. Although they had not intended to make new lives on the night they had slept together, they had, indeed, made two little new lives.

Instead of following through on his inappropriate impulse to pull her into his arms, he smiled and stuck his hands in his pockets. "You'll let me know if there's anything else you need for in here?"

"Trust me, there isn't a thing more I need."

"Then I think it's time I get out of here so you can get some rest."

They walked back down the hall and to the front door. "Thanks for the coffee."

"Anytime," she replied.

"How about tomorrow evening I pick you up and take you to my place? I'll provide the meal."

She frowned. "That means you will have paid for my dinner twice."

"Avery, do we really have to keep score?"

"No, we don't," she replied with a laugh. "And I'd love to go to your place tomorrow evening."

"Great, then how about I pick you up around five?"

"Sounds perfect to me."

Minutes later he was in his truck and headed home. Home was the Colton ranch, over a thousand acres of rich, fertile pastureland owned by his father, Hays, and his mother, Josephine.

When he'd gotten out of the army and returned here, he'd laid claim to an old foreman's cabin, which had needed lots of repairs. The hard work had been welcome to keep his mind off the pain of loss that still ached in his heart. When he wasn't helping with search and rescue, he'd worked on the old place until it had become a decent space to call home.

Now all he could think about was how he needed to turn the small spare bedroom there into a nursery of his own. He'd need two cribs and all the items it took to keep two babies healthy and happy.

Although he and Avery hadn't even touched on the custody issue yet, he wanted to share the babies from the moment they were born. It was important he bond with them right from the get-go. He only hoped Avery would be on the same page as him when it came to custody.

Avery. There was still so much he had to learn about her, but he'd enjoyed his time with her tonight far more than he'd anticipated. He found her so easy to talk to, and with a great sense of humor. He hadn't expected that.

He pulled up in front of the cabin, where he'd been living for the past three months since he'd returned to Whisperwood from his base in Houston.

The cozy place was sheltered from the winds by

tall trees on either side, and there was a small porch on the back that faced more woods. It was not only a quiet, peaceful place, but was also a bit isolated, which he didn't mind.

When he'd first come home, his grief still a living, breathing thing inside him, he hadn't wanted to be around people except those who needed him in the rescue efforts. But with his family it was impossible to stay isolated for long. They absolutely wouldn't allow it.

He parked his truck in front and then went inside. He turned on an end table lamp and instantly his gaze fell on a framed photo of Ivy.

She was in her army uniform and she appeared to be gazing at him in silent accusation. He sank down on the brown leather recliner and picked up the photo.

It had been a little over a year since her death, and yet the pain of her loss felt as fresh as if she had died yesterday. He'd known her for three months before they had gotten married. Some people might have said they rushed things, but he had known it was right on the day he had met her. They had been married for three years when she'd been killed.

They'd dreamed of creating a family together. The plan had been that once both of them were out of uniform for good they would buy a house and work on making their first baby. But an IED in Afghanistan, where Ivy had been serving her last tour of duty, had ended not only their hopes and dreams, but also her life.

He ran a finger over Ivy's face in the picture. Her short brown hair emphasized her big, soulful brown eyes. "I have to get along with her," he whispered to her. "Avery is nothing more than the mother of my children. You have my heart, Ivy, and you'll always have it."

He set the picture back on the end table. He hoped he and Avery could become good friends for the sake of the babies. But there would never again be a woman in his life who was anything more than a friend, because his heart had been buried along with his wife.

Chapter 3

Avery was in the kitchen at four thirty the next afternoon when the phone rang, and seeing the caller identification, she smiled as she answered. "Hey, girlfriend."

"Hey, yourself," Breanna Wallace replied. "What's happening?"

Breanna was one of Avery's close friends, so close that she knew all about the night the twins had been conceived and who Avery had fallen into bed with.

"A lot," Avery replied. She told her about meeting Dallas at the courthouse, and that they were now working on building a friendship that would serve the twins well.

"Wow, I'd like to be hanging out with a man as hot

as Dallas Colton," Breanna replied. "Instead I've got a two-year-old son who has decided being naked is wonderful, a four-year-old daughter who wants mac and cheese for every meal, and an ex-husband who is paying for his girlfriend's breast augmentation, but is four months late on his child support." She stopped and drew a deep, audible breath. "Whew, that was a mouthful and I now want details about you and Dallas."

Avery laughed. "There aren't a lot of details to tell you. We went out to dinner together last night and tonight he's taking me to his place."

"His place, huh? Any romantic sparks flying between you two?" Breanna asked. "According to what you told me, sparks definitely flew on the night you met."

"No," Avery replied quickly. "That's not what we're looking for. We just need to build a strong friendship between us so we can effectively coparent together." Avery didn't want to think about the moments that Dallas's smile had shot a wave of heat through her, or the way her heart quickened its beat in his presence.

She watched Lulu disappear out the doggie door and then glanced at the clock on the microwave. In twenty minutes the object of their conversation would be here to pick her up. Thankfully, she was ready to go and so had a few more minutes to visit with Breanna.

They continued to catch up with each other until Avery had to call a halt. "Breanna, I need to go. Dallas will be here any time to pick me up."

"Go and have a good time," Breanna replied. "And I want details tomorrow." As they ended the call Lulu came back into the house and danced directly to the drawer under the microwave where Avery kept her treats. She stared at the drawer and then looked at Avery. She rose up on her back legs and released a bark.

"Okay," Avery said with a laugh. She got up from the kitchen chair and gave Lulu a treat, and then went into the living room to wait for Dallas.

Despite what she'd told Breanna about this being strictly a mission of building a friendship, she couldn't help the way her heart beat a bit faster in anticipation of seeing Dallas again. She wanted to like him, just not to like him in any kind of a romantic way.

After Zeke's death she had decided she was good living alone. If she hadn't gotten pregnant when she had, eventually she probably would have checked into artificial insemination or adoption.

She could raise her children and give them all the love in her heart, but beyond her babies, she never wanted to care that deeply about another human being again. She would forever shield her heart from that kind of hurt, as best she could. Love outside her children wasn't an option in her life.

She was eager to see where Dallas lived. He'd said it was an old cabin. What kind of shape was it in? She didn't care how he lived, but if he took the babies for his turn at custody, she needed to make sure the place was clean and safe and appropriate.

As she saw Dallas's truck turning onto her street, she bent down and stroked her hands down little Lulu's back. The length of the soft, curly black fur reminded her that it was past time to take the dog to the groomers.

"You be a good little girl while I'm gone, and I'll be back later," she said, and then she grabbed her purse and opened her front door.

She stepped out at the same time Dallas got out of his truck. He walked around to the passenger side and opened the door for her, and then turned to greet her with that wonderful smile of his. "How are you?"

"I'm good," she replied, and slid into the passenger seat. He closed the door and then walked around the front of the truck to his side.

He looked as handsome as she'd ever seen him. He wore a pair of blue jeans that looked like they'd been especially made to fit his long legs and tight butt. The navy T-shirt showcased his broad shoulders and arm muscles. There was no question the man was hot.

He got into the truck, bringing with him the scent of sunshine and his clean, fresh cologne. "You look nice," he said, as he started the engine.

"Thank you." She ran her hands down the rose-and-black blouse. "I have a rather limited wardrobe now."

He turned to look at her. "Do you need more clothes? I could buy you—"

"Dallas," she interrupted. "I refuse to buy another maternity blouse this close to giving birth. You just might have to deal with seeing me in the same blouse more than once."

"I can deal with that," he replied. "So, how was your day?" he asked once they were on the road.

"It was good, although I have to confess I was a bit of a slug. I slept sinfully late and then I read for most of the afternoon. I did absolutely nothing constructive all day. What about you?"

"Normally I would have been out with the other men doing cleanup on some of the properties that suffered flood damage. But knowing I was having a visitor this evening, I did some cleaning and then went into town and did some shopping."

"Oh, I hope you haven't gone to a lot of trouble," she said.

"I only did what needed to be done," he replied. "Are you hungry?"

"Always," she replied with a laugh.

"I hope you like steak."

"I love a good steak," she replied.

"What else do you love when it comes to food?"

"I like Mexican and some Chinese, I love pizza and barbecue and I would never turn down a fried chicken drumstick. What about you?" She supposed this was part of the getting to know each other that built a friendship.

"It would be easier to tell you what I don't like. Brussel sprouts and liver."

She laughed. "We definitely agree on that, and I will never force the children to eat those two foods."

"That's good to know," he replied.

"But I will insist they eat other vegetables and meat."

"And I'll occasionally sneak them a piece of candy."

Once again they shared laughter and then they fell silent as he left town and continued to head in the direction of the Colton ranch. It was a comfortable silence that she felt no need to fill. Rather, she directed her gaze out the passenger window, watching the passing scenery.

So far she found him very agreeable, but they hadn't really had the hard conversations yet. Talking about favorite foods and sharing a few laughs over their daily life was all fine and good, but she knew there were more difficult conversations to come.

But nothing had to be sorted out immediately. There was still a month and a half before the babies were actually due to arrive. Right now she just wanted to enjoy spending time with him, and work on a friendship that would make the more difficult conversations a little easier.

They began to pass pastureland. "It's so beautiful out here," she said.

"As far as I'm concerned this is the prettiest place on the face of the earth."

"I'm sure you saw some pretty grim places in your military life."

A knot formed in his jaw and pulsed for a moment before he replied. "Yes, I did. I don't really like to talk about my military life. I'm definitely glad I got out when I did, otherwise I wouldn't have been at the courthouse here in town to run into you and discover I'm going to be a father."

"Strange how that worked out, isn't it?"

He smiled at her. "A bit of serendipity at work."

Serendipity…good fortune…a twist of fate. Whatever it had been, she was just glad that things had worked out the way they had. At least she knew the twins would have a father in their lives. And hopefully he would be a good father, unlike the distant and busy one who had been in her own life.

She relaxed back into the seat. Once again a silence fell between them, but as before, it was a comfortable one. She'd been relaxed all day as she'd slowly processed the fact that there would be no more going to work every day for some time to come. She loved her work, but she was looking forward to being a stay-at-home mom for the next couple months.

They turned off onto the Colton property and drove past the nice house where Josephine and Hays lived. They continued down a dirt road that led them deeper onto the property. They passed several outbuildings before a wooded area appeared, along with a small cabin.

He pulled up and parked in front of it. She got out of the truck and looked around with interest. The only sounds were the faint breeze whispering through the trees, the songs of birds and, from someplace in the distance, a cow mooed.

"What a peaceful place," she said.

"It is peaceful," he agreed. "Let's see if it passes the mommy test for a place to bring the twins." He opened the door and ushered her inside.

She entered into a nice living room with a neat and clean kitchenette on one side. The overstuffed, brown leather furniture and the stone fireplace invited a guest to sit and relax.

There was a desk against one wall with a computer open on top and papers and other items on one side. The whole room held an implied warmth and welcome, and a cleanliness that was comforting to her.

"This is really nice, Dallas. When you said a cabin in the woods, I wasn't sure exactly what to expect, but this is quite lovely."

"Thanks. Let me show you the rest of it." He led her to a doorway on the right. He opened the door to a bedroom that held a king-size bed with a black-and-gray spread, dresser drawers and two end tables with small lamps.

"Very nice," she commented.

He closed the door and then gestured to the next one. "This is the bathroom." He then opened the third one and she walked into a nursery.

It was a small room, but it was almost the mirror image of what she had in her house. There were two cribs, one with blue bedding and one with pink. The only thing really different was the mobiles that hung over each crib. Where she had dancing bears, he had little horses.

Unexpected emotion surged up inside her. The room showed her that he was really serious about being a part of the twins' lives. The room was a promise both to her and the babies she carried that he intended to be a part of their future.

"When did you manage to do all this?" she asked, speaking around the lump in her throat.

"Today." He flashed that devastating grin of his. "I took the day off to try to catch up with you."

"It looks like you definitely managed to catch up with me," she replied. It truly was a promise that he intended to stick around, and it made her feel closer to him.

"Why don't we go back into the living room and I'll start dinner."

"Sounds good to me," she replied. Instead of sitting on the sofa, she took a seat at the table for two, which was already set with plates, silverware and drink glasses. "Is there anything I can do to help?"

"I've got the grill outside ready to go so all you need to do is tell me how you like your steak."

"That's easy. Medium rare."

"Ah, a woman after my own heart. I'm going to take the steaks outside to cook. I'll be right back."

She was almost glad he'd stepped outside because

all of a sudden her brain was filled with memories of the night they had shared together.

She remembered the fire of his kisses and the sweet slide of his naked body against hers. His touches had absolutely enflamed her. Even though she'd had too much to drink, it had been the hottest, most intense lovemaking she'd ever had in her entire life.

And why, oh why, was she thinking about it right now? It had to be out-of-whack pregnancy hormones. Memories of that night had nothing to do with the relationship they were building right now, other than the consequences that had occurred. She had to put memories of that night with him out of her mind for good.

She turned in the chair and gazed around the cozy room, trying to change the direction of her thoughts. This was definitely a place her babies could come and spend time in without any concerns.

Was Dallas really in this for the long run? He had created the perfect nursery, a commitment for sure. But babies were like new toys. They were fun to play with for a while, but was it possible Dallas would lose interest as days turned into months and months into years?

Only time would tell.

Along with the steaks, Dallas had prepared a salad and baked potatoes. "This all looks wonderful," Avery said, once he had everything on the table.

"This is one of the easiest meals for a man to make. Fling some lettuce into a bowl, toss a couple of potatoes in the oven and throw the meat on a grill."

She laughed. "I'm sure a little more went into this meal than what you just described."

He liked the sound of her melodious laughter. She looked particularly pretty tonight, clad in a rose-colored blouse and a pair of black slacks. There was no question that she was hugely pregnant, but he was surprised to realize he still found her very attractive. Maybe it was because he knew she carried his children.

"Have you thought about names?" he asked.

"Yes, I have. After giving it a lot of thought, I'm leaning toward Fred and Ethel."

He stared at her, momentarily rendered speechless. Was she serious? Fred and Ethel? She wanted to name his children after a couple in a sitcom from the fifties?

She burst out laughing. "Oh, I wish I had gotten a picture of your expression just now."

"So, you aren't really serious about Fred and Ethel?"

"So not serious," she replied with another laugh. "Actually, for the last month I've been trying to decide on names, but so far I haven't been able to pick two. Now it's something we can decide on together."

His heart swelled. "I'd like that. You know, I have to admit that there's still a part of me that finds this all a little hard to believe."

She gazed at him, her green eyes suddenly dark and solemn. "Dallas, I'd be glad to get a DNA test after the babies are born."

"Oh God, Avery, that's not what I meant and I don't need that from you." He reached across the table and took her hand in his, afraid that he'd offended her unintentionally. "What I meant was that one minute I was a single man standing in front of the courthouse and the next minute I was a father-to-be to not one, but two babies."

She smiled and pulled her hand from his. "You're still a single man. You can date, and that's something that hasn't changed."

"But it has," he protested. "I have absolutely no desire to date at the moment. All I want is to spend time with you and get to know you better. I want to go to your doctor appointments with you and support you and be an integral part of this amazing experience."

"I appreciate that, and speaking of doctor appointments, I have one on Monday at two in the afternoon."

"Then I'd like to take you, if that's okay."

Once again she smiled. "It's more than okay with me."

For the next few minutes they ate and talked about their views of discipline. He was grateful that they seemed to be on the same page.

They both preferred time-outs to spankings. They

believed that open communication was key and keeping strong boundaries and a united front was vital.

"Have you thought about how we should handle the custody issue?" she asked.

"I would definitely like equal custody," he replied. "But we can worry about the details later."

She nodded and then set her fork down. "I am stuffed. This was a wonderful meal."

"I hope you aren't too stuffed for dessert," he replied.

She grinned. "I could probably force myself to eat a little dessert."

"Good, then why don't you go relax on the sofa and I'll get it ready." He got up from the table.

She stood and picked up her empty plate. "At least let me help with the cleanup."

"Absolutely not. You are my guest tonight and I insist you go sit and relax." He took the plate from her. "Please."

"If you don't mind I'll just wander around the room a bit." She placed her hands on her lower back and winced.

He looked at her with concern. "Are you okay?"

"I'm fine. I just need to stretch a little bit. These kids sometimes ride low in my back."

As he cleaned up the kitchen, he was aware of her walking around the living room. She stopped by his desk. "What are these?" she asked.

Immediately he knew what she was looking at.

He placed the last plate in the dishwasher and then joined her by the desk, where three buttons with unusual markings sat next to his computer. "These were found next to Patrice Eccleston's body. Do you know about the case?"

"A little, but not much. I was pretty much kept out of the loop due to my condition and the fact that I was going on maternity leave."

"So, what do you know?" he asked.

"Just that her body was found in the Lone Star Pharma parking lot when they were digging it up due to renovations. I didn't know her personally, but I do know she was twenty years old and is part of an ongoing investigation. What don't I know?"

"There was evidence that she was bound and that she struggled before she was killed. These buttons were found near her body and the same kind of buttons were found near the mummified body recently found at Maggie Reeves's house."

Maggie Reeves was a former beauty queen and cotillion champ, but recently a fully mummified skeleton of a young woman had been found on the outskirts of Live Oak Ranch. Dallas's oldest brother, Jonah, had helped Maggie investigate and the two had fallen in love. Still, that mummified body hadn't been the end of the investigation, for Patrice's body had then been found.

Avery grimaced. "I can't believe we're talking about the mummy murders again. I thought that was behind us and they were solved when Elliot Corgan was tried and convicted."

Approximately forty years ago, seven young women had gone missing. Police finally found all the bodies except one, buried in ditches with red scarves stuffed in their mouths. Because of the condition of the bodies, the killer was dubbed the Mummy Killer.

Elliot Corgan, the brother of a successful rancher in Whisperwood, was arrested for the crimes. And now mummified bodies had shown up again in the small town.

"We all had hoped that when Elliot was arrested that would be the end of it," he replied. "But now there's a lot of doubt about who might have been responsible for the murders that occurred forty years ago, and who is responsible for those happening now."

"So, what are you doing with the buttons?" she asked. She stared at them with a frown and he wondered if he should have told her as much as he had. The last thing he wanted was for her to think about murder and mummified bodies while in her condition.

"The buttons went to the lab, where they tried to lift some DNA evidence, but whatever might have been there was too disintegrated. The forensic specialist, Dr. Octavia Winters, identified them as army standard uniform buttons, so I've been asked to do some research to try to find army men who were stationed locally around forty years ago."

"Wow, that's going to take some work. Texas isn't short on army bases and I'm sure the records from that long ago aren't all that good." She turned to look at him, a light of excitement in her eyes. "I could help you with this research, Dallas."

"You don't need to get involved with any of this," he replied.

"Dallas, I want to get involved. Since I'm not working right now I have all the time in the world to sit at my computer and help." She looked at him pleadingly. "Please let me do this."

"Okay," he said, relenting. "To be honest, I could use some help with the project. I've asked around to get names from people who remember soldiers from that time frame, but now I'm doing internet searches."

They sat on the sofa and for the next few minutes he told her what sites needed to be checked out to get the names of soldiers. "Unfortunately, you're right, records from forty years ago aren't that easy to find," he said.

"If it helps get a killer off the streets then I'm definitely in on helping however I can," she replied.

"I just hate like hell to believe any fellow soldier might be involved in these horrific crimes," he said.

"Soldiers are people, Dallas, and most of them are upstanding and dedicated. But sometimes some people do terrible things."

"Yeah, I guess you're right, but I still hate to believe

a soldier is responsible. Now, enough about all this. You sit tight and I'm going to go get your dessert."

He got up and went back to the kitchen area. He was glad her back was to him so she couldn't see what he was doing. He first pulled out the cherry pie he'd bought at the store and cut them each a piece. He topped the pie with whipped cream and then moved on to prepare the dessert he intended to give her before the pie.

When he had it ready, he carried the plate into the living room and set it on the coffee table before her. She stared at the jar of green olives next to the bag of salt-and-vinegar potato chips and then threw back her head and laughed.

He found himself laughing with her. It felt good. He didn't feel like he'd really laughed for the past year. They both sobered and the gaze she sent him was filled with warmth.

"My favorite dessert," she said.

"Actually, that's your take-home dessert. I'll be right back with the real one." He was almost grateful to escape for a minute. Because for just a moment he'd wanted to fall into the warmth in her beautiful green eyes. For just a moment he'd wanted to pull her into an embrace and taste her lips once again.

And that made him angry.

It should be Ivy sitting in his cabin. It should be Ivy carrying his children. It should be his wife he laughed with, and her tempting him with her lush lips. Damn fate for taking her away from him.

And damn him for even thinking for one second about kissing Avery.

Chapter 4

Avery awoke late on Sunday morning. She'd tossed and turned for half the night with the babies doing what felt like hip-hop dances in her belly. She'd also had heartburn and the combination of the two had kept her awake and uncomfortable for several agonizing hours.

If that wasn't enough, thoughts of Dallas had whirled in her brain, confusing thoughts that had concerned her. She'd really enjoyed the evening with him, but by the time he brought her home things had become awkward between them.

She felt as if he'd rushed her when she'd eaten the cherry pie, and then he'd immediately taken her home. He'd grown quiet and closed off, making her wonder if she'd done something wrong. And she'd tossed and turned, with her brain working overtime, to try to figure out what that might have been, but hadn't been able to come up with anything.

They'd made no plans for today, but he'd told her he'd pick her up tomorrow for her two o'clock doctor appointment. Maybe it was good for them not to see each other today. Just because he was here now and they were working on building a friendship didn't mean they had to be together 24/7.

She pulled herself out of bed and then showered and slipped on a long navy blue dress that hugged her breasts and then skimmed the rest of her body. It was one of the most comfortable articles of clothing for her right now.

She was eating breakfast when her phone rang. She looked at the caller identification and cursed herself. She'd completely forgotten to call Danny back.

"Hey, Chad," she said.

"Hi, Avery. Danny and I were wondering if we could bring lunch to you and visit for a little while."

"That would be nice, and please tell Danny I'm sorry I haven't called him back. Things have been a little crazy for me the last couple of days."

"No problem. Would right around noon work for you?"

"That would be fine with me," she replied. "I look forward to seeing you both."

She hung up with a smile. Visiting with Chad

and Danny was always pleasant. The two men had been like overly protective brothers to her for the last several months. They hadn't let her carry anything heavier than a file folder in the office and had even followed her home to unload groceries and the like.

After she cleaned up her breakfast dishes she sat at her desk in her home office and pulled up her email. There was really nothing that needed her attention. She then checked her other social media and laughed at several funny memes Breanna had posted to her.

She pulled up one of the websites Dallas had given her to search for soldiers who had been stationed in the area forty some years ago.

She was glad Dallas had agreed to let her help. There was nothing she'd love more than to get a murderer off the streets. And for the next month or so, until she delivered, she had nothing but time on her hands.

Despite what a slug she'd been the day before, she preferred to be productive, and wasn't the type to sit around doing nothing day after day.

Hopefully, she would be able to find some names of potential suspects in the horrific murders that had occurred in the town.

There was something terrible going on in Whisperwood, something tied to the murders that had happened years ago. But so far the authorities were baffled. Those old army buttons showing up at the latest crime scenes were definitely disturbing.

She was still seated at her computer when her doorbell rang. She was shocked to look at the nearby clock and realize it was just after noon. She hurried to the front door and opened it to the two men.

Chad swept in first. He was a tall man, distinguished looking with premature salt-and-pepper hair. His blue eyes were soft and warm as he greeted her, but she'd seen them go gas-flame intense when he was before a jury and attacking a defendant.

Chad had gone through a divorce six months before and was now hitting the dating scene hard. His penchant seemed to be for young, vacuous blondes with big breasts, the exact opposite of his dark-haired former wife.

The shorter, much shyer Danny followed behind him and carried two large take-out bags from the diner. He walked to the kitchen table and began to unload the contents.

"Oh my gosh, it looks like you two bought way too much food," she said.

Danny smiled at her. "You know how Chad can eat."

"Damn right," Chad said. "It takes a lot of fuel to keep me this good-looking and awesome."

"And humble," Avery replied with a laugh. "We can't forget how humble you are."

Within minutes the three of them were at the table

with full plates before them. The two men were not only caring coworkers, but had also become close friends. When they had realized she was pregnant and all alone, they had taken her under their wings.

They had been the ones who had helped her set up the cribs. They had carried in boxes of diapers from her car, Danny had even driven her to a doctor appointment when she hadn't been feeling well enough to drive herself.

Chad often referred to Danny as his younger brother from another mother. The two couldn't be more different. Where Chad was outgoing and a whole lot of confident bluster, Danny was much quieter and with a sweetness that made him a favorite among everyone at the office.

"Danny, I'm sorry I didn't call you back the other day," she said, and then popped a french fry into her mouth.

"No problem. I just wanted to check in with you."

"He worries about you," Chad said.

Danny shot Chad a look of irritation and then gazed back at her. "Of course I worry about you. You're my friend."

"Thanks, Danny. I appreciate it, and as you can see, I'm doing fine, just getting bigger and bigger every day." She laughed and placed a hand on her belly.

"As long as you and the babies are healthy, that's all that's important," he replied.

"Since I haven't really been gone from work yet for any length of time, I guess there's no news for you two to share with me," she said. Chad and Danny exchanged a quick glance. "What?" She looked from one man to the other. "What is it?"

"Actually, there is something I heard. Apparently some of Dwayne Conway's thug friends are talking trash about wanting revenge for him going to jail," Chad said.

"We thought you needed to know," Danny said, his brown eyes holding her gaze for a long moment before he shyly looked away.

"But you know how these creeps are," Chad said dismissively. "After a trial when one of them gets locked up, the rest whine and talk trash for about a week, and then they get back to their low-life ways."

"Still, we thought it was important you know about the threats," Danny added.

"I've had threats against me before and have managed to survive," she replied.

"Still, I want you to call me if anything happens that scares you." Danny's gaze again held hers for a moment and then once again skittered away.

"Thanks, Danny. I appreciate that, but I'm sure I'll be fine."

"We don't want any of those creeps bothering you," Chad added.

"I've really appreciated all the things you two

have done to help me, but you're officially off the hook now," she replied.

"What does that mean?" Chad asked.

"The daddy is back in the picture." She explained to them that the baby's father had come back into town after being gone for months and that the two of them were now working on building a relationship of friendship.

When she was finished, Chad looked at his friend. "Well, Danny, old boy, it sounds like we're being tossed out with the morning trash."

Avery laughed in protest. "You know that isn't true. I love having the two of you in my life and I hope both of you will continue to be part of it. These babies could always use uncles."

The rest of the lunch passed uneventfully, with them talking about past trials and some that Chad anticipated happening in the future.

By two o'clock she was once again alone in her house. As she sank back down at the computer to work, she thought about what Chad had told her about Dwayne Conway's friends threatening some sort of revenge against her.

It didn't really scare her. It was probably all a bunch of big bark and no bite. Those kind of thugs enjoyed making threats, but Avery didn't anticipate them actually following through and doing anything. Besides, she was no longer working at the office so the bunch of dope-selling thugs would probably focus their attention on one of the other prosecutors.

By the time she knocked off working on the computer she'd found only one name for Dallas. She wished she'd found more, but the work was very tedious and difficult.

For dinner she ate some of the leftovers Chad and Danny hadn't taken with them when they had gone. The house was quiet, and now that her brain wasn't engaged doing much of anything, it filled with thoughts of Dallas.

It was funny how a week ago she hadn't spent a minute of time with Dallas in months, and hadn't even known he was back in Whisperwood. But this evening she realized she'd missed seeing him today. It had to be a result of her crazy pregnancy hormones again.

Certainly she couldn't expect any real relationship with him, nor did she want one. Now that he was here, all she wanted from him was to be a good father to his children.

Still, she couldn't help the way her heart danced the next afternoon when he pulled up in her driveway to take her to her doctor appointment.

"Be back soon, sweet baby," she said to Lulu, and then she left the house.

His smile warmed her from head to toe as he greeted her. She slid into the passenger seat and wondered if it was so wrong that just being around him brought her pleasure. That being in his presence made her feel strangely safe and secure. Surely it wasn't wrong to feel that way about a man who would be in her children's lives? In fact, it had to be good that she felt that way about him.

"How was your day yesterday?" he asked, once they were on the road.

"It was good. I had lunch with a couple of coworkers." She told him about Chad and Danny and how they had helped her so much, especially during the past couple months. She told him about them being responsible for the shower that had taken place at work and how they checked in with her often to make sure she was doing okay.

"I'd like to meet them. I definitely appreciate everything they did for you while I wasn't around," he replied. He cast her a quick glance. "Maybe they have a crush on you."

"What on earth would make you think they have a crush on me?"

"You are a very attractive woman, Avery."

She laughed. "Thanks, but no way. Chad is divorced and has become the biggest womanizer you ever want to meet. He likes his women blonde and dumb. He would never have any kind of a crush on me. I probably remind him of his ex-wife, and he hates her."

"And what about this Danny?" Dallas asked.

She started to reply with a firm "no way," but instead took a minute to think about the sweet, shy, dark-haired man. "I suppose it is possible Danny might have a little crush on me, but I've never done anything to encourage him and he's never spoken to me about it. He's so shy it's hard to know what he's feeling about much of anything."

"It's really none of my business. I was just curious," he replied. "I like to know about anyone who is going to be in the twins' lives."

"I understand that and I feel the same way about wanting to know who is going to be around when they are at your place," she replied.

For the rest of the ride to the doctor's office they spoke about the weather and other inconsequential things. She was just grateful that Dallas displayed none of the quiet, closed-off man she'd seen at the end of their time together on Saturday evening.

She still didn't know what had happened that night and wondered if he was just a moody kind of man. It was a reminder that there was still a lot to learn about each other.

By the time they reached Dr. Julia Sanders's office, excitement about her appointment began to bubble inside her. She knew the doctor would be doing an ultrasound and Avery was always eager to see pictures of her babies. It was also exciting that for the first time she wouldn't be experiencing it all alone.

She couldn't begin to count the minutes she had

sat in the waiting room amid happy couples sharing the experience.

Today she was finally with the father of her children, and for the first time since she'd been coming to the office, they were the only ones in the waiting room.

Dallas stood right behind her as she checked in at the receptionist's desk, then they took seats side by side to wait to be called back to the examining rooms.

"Do you like the doctor?" Dallas asked softly.

"I love her. She's relatively new to town and I've been so impressed with her I've recommended her to several of my friends and coworkers. I not only like her, but I trust her."

"That's good," he replied. "I would assume it's important for a pregnant woman to trust her doctor."

"I think it's important for anyone to like and trust their doctor," she replied.

"You said she's new to town. Where does she come from?" he asked.

"She's originally from Whisperwood but went to medical school in Kansas City. She had a thriving practice there, but when her parents got ill a year ago she moved back here."

Before they could say anything else, the nurse called her name. Once in the examining room Dallas sat on a chair in the corner while Avery sat on the edge of the padded table.

The nurse, Jennifer Malkin, took Avery's blood

pressure, her temperature and her pulse. After charting the results, she told them the doctor would be in soon and then left the room.

"It's a good thing she didn't take my blood pressure because I'm sure it isn't normal right now," Dallas said.

Avery smiled at him. "So, you're excited to be here?"

"Nervous...excited...anxious..." His voice drifted off and he changed positions in the plastic chair.

At that moment Dr. Sanders walked in. Her gray-blonde hair was cut in a pixie style that emphasized her big blue eyes and delicate features.

Avery introduced Dallas and the doctor greeted him with a delighted smile. "So, Daddy is finally here. Do you plan on being in the delivery room when these precious babies make their debuts?"

He shot a panicked look at Avery. "Uh...we haven't really talked about that yet."

"Really?" The doctor looked at them both in surprise. "Well, it's something you should probably decide fairly soon. Before you know it these babies are going to make their appearance."

For the next few minutes Dr. Sanders asked Avery questions about her general health. Once the inquiries were over she asked her to lie on the examining bed. "Now, let's get a look and a listen of those babies."

The nurse came in to assist, and helped Avery lift the navy blouse she was wearing to the bottom of her bra and then push her pants down low enough to bare her belly. Even though nothing really private was showing, Avery was suddenly shy, with Dallas in the room and her belly completely exposed.

"Come on, Daddy. Pull that chair up here next to your woman," Dr. Sanders instructed. "Surely you want to get a good view of these babies you created."

Dallas moved his chair to Avery's side and offered her what appeared to be an awkward smile. And that smile made his presence next to her something wonderful.

"Let's take a listen first." The doctor placed a special stethoscope on Avery's stomach and instantly the sound of a heartbeat could be heard. "Ah, there's mama's heartbeat, nice and strong. Let's see what else we can find in here." She moved the instrument around and suddenly two more heartbeats could be heard. "There they are…"

Avery looked at Dallas. His eyes were wide, and he grinned. "And they sound okay?" he asked.

"They sound exactly like they are supposed to, nice and healthy," Dr. Sanders replied. She took off the stethoscope and squirted some warm gel on Avery's stomach. "Now, let's take a peek."

She began to move the wand around on Avery's bulging belly and all three of them looked at the screen on the machine.

Dallas gasped as the image of two little beings appeared. The little boy was curled around the little girl, as if already showing himself to be a protective brother. The sweet baby girl was sucking her thumb. Dallas grabbed Avery's hand and a well of emotion surged inside her chest.

For just a moment she felt a closeness with him that even transcended the night they had made love. For just a brief, crazy moment she wished he was in love with her and they would go home together and plan their life as a family.

With his hand tightly clasped around hers as they looked at the children they had made, she wanted him to be in her life not just as her babies' father, but also as the man who loved her.

As Dallas heard the two little heartbeats fill the air and saw the picture of the two babies, his heart expanded to a capacity so great he couldn't speak. Tears blurred his vision as he stared at the screen where the twins appeared.

They were his children and he already loved them more than he'd ever loved another soul in his entire life. He'd never known he could love like this.

He was determined to be the very best man he could be for them. He would protect them from any and all danger, and he would be the absolute best father he knew how to be.

He released Avery's hand and smiled at her. He would always care for Avery, because she was the mother of his children. But if there ever came a time when he believed she was doing something that wasn't in their best interest, then he would fight her tooth and nail.

Minutes later he and Avery walked out of the doctor's office. He now had a photo of the twins in his pocket and the assurance from the doctor that the babies appeared to be doing well. Dallas was feeling on top of the world.

"I think we need to do something to celebrate," he said, once they were in his truck.

"What do you have in mind?" she asked.

"Ice cream. What do you think about going to Edwards's Ice Cream Parlor and indulging in a big sundae or cone?"

She laughed. "Oh, Dallas, you're definitely speaking my language."

"All right then." He started the truck and headed to Main Street, where the small shop sold ice cream in dozens of flavors.

"I'm so glad the doctor said that Hansel and Gretel are thriving and doing well," he said, knowing it would make her laugh. And it did.

He enjoyed the sound of her musical laughter. At the moment he felt as if he would enjoy anything she said or did. And she'd never looked more beautiful.

She was wearing a navy blouse with a light blue stripe down the sides, and navy slacks. Her hair glittered with the sunshine that drifted through the truck window. He knew he was riding an emotional high after seeing the images of his babies thriving in her stomach. And that high made her the most beautiful and enchanting creature on the face of the earth.

"Do you really think I'm going to be good with burdening the children with names like Hansel and Gretel?" she asked. "Besides, didn't they end up in a witch's oven?"

"I really don't remember my fairy tales very well. It was just a thought," he said teasingly. "And it's definitely better than Fred and Ethel."

"I agree, but I think you need to keep on thinking," she replied, and laughed once again.

They arrived at Edward's and together entered the store, which sported a long counter, high parlor tables and chairs, and pink-and-white-striped wallpaper.

"Order whatever you want," he said to her. "Be as self-indulgent as you want to be."

"Trust me, put me in an ice cream shop and I can be very, very self-indulgent."

Walt Edwards greeted them with a cheerful smile. "You two look like a couple of ice cream lovers to me."

"You've got that right," Dallas replied. "She needs enough ice cream for three."

Walt's bushy eyebrows danced upward as he looked at Avery. "Ah, twins! What a blessing for the two of you."

"Yes, it is," Dallas agreed.

"What can I get for you?" he asked Avery.

"I'd like a hot fudge sundae with extra hot fudge and whipped cream," she replied, and then looked sheepishly at Dallas. "You said for me to indulge."

He grinned reassuringly at her. "Go for it."

She turned back to Walt. "Okay, then add sprinkles…lots and lots of sprinkles."

"You got it," Walt replied.

"And I'll have a banana split," Dallas said.

"Have a seat at one of the tables and I'll bring them out to you," Walt replied.

They chose a table near the window and settled in, and within minutes had their ice cream concoctions in front of them.

She took a bite of hers and moaned deep in the back of her throat. A sudden, sharp, sexual desire spiked through Dallas. She'd made that same sound when he'd made love to her.

Suddenly his mind was filled with memories of that night. Her skin had been so soft and her body so welcoming. Her lips had been hot and eager beneath his. They had moved together as if they'd been lovers for years and knew from long practice what the other needed to heighten the pleasure.

He stared down at his ice cream as the erotic memories continued to race through his brain. He was shocked to realize he wouldn't mind going there again with her. Not that he would… That would be unfair to her because he had no interest in having any kind of long-term romantic relationship with her other than as a coparent.

"Dallas?"

Her voice pulled him from his thoughts and he looked up at her. She gave him an uncertain smile. "Is everything okay?"

He realized he'd been lost in his own head for several minutes. She'd eaten half her sundae, while his banana split was melting into a puddle of goo in front of him.

"Sorry," he said, and smiled. "I guess I got caught up in trying to think of alternatives to Hansel and Gretel."

"We still have plenty of time to settle on the absolute perfect names for them," she replied.

"I still can't get over being able to see them."

She nodded. "It's amazing, isn't it? I'm just so grateful they are both about the same size. Dr. Sanders said sometimes with twins one is larger than the other and takes more of the nutrition."

"Then it's good to know they're already sharing nicely," he replied.

She stirred her spoon through the last of her ice cream. "I know you've set up a nursery in the cabin, but I'll be honest with you…" She paused and stared down at the table, as if afraid to say what was on her mind.

"What, Avery? You'll be honest with me about what?" A faint tension filled his chest. Was she going to tell him he couldn't have the twins at his place? That certainly was going to cause a major issue between them.

She gazed at him once again. "I'd like to have the babies full-time at my house for the first eight weeks or so. I want to work out a reasonable custody plan with you," she hurriedly added. "I just hate to have them taken out in those first weeks."

"Actually, I agree with you about that," he replied with relief. "As long as I can come over and spend time with them in those first few weeks, I'm good with them being at your house."

She visibly relaxed. "Thank you. I just don't like the idea of them being shuttled back and forth between your house and mine as newborns. And of course during that time you'll be welcome to spend as much time at my place as you want."

"Thanks. I'm glad we're definitely on the same page with that," he agreed.

She offered him a wide smile. "I like it when we're on the same page about things."

"Me, too."

They finished their ice cream and got into his truck to head back to her house. "You want to come in for a cup of coffee?" she asked, when he pulled up in the driveway.

"That sounds good." It had been such a wonderful day, starting with the ultrasound. He was reluctant to see it all come to an end.

Lulu greeted them as they walked in, dancing around their feet and barking her happiness. Dallas laughed and picked up the wiggling ball of black fur.

"How is this little princess going to cope with Mommy having two new babies in the house?" he asked.

"She'll be fine," she replied as she led him into the kitchen. "She has been around some of my friends' babies and she loves them. I don't see any problems looming with Lulu and the new kids in the house."

He set Lulu on the floor and she immediately disappeared out the doggie door. Dallas sat in one of the chairs at the table while Avery made him a cup of coffee and herself a cup of tea.

He was pleased that he was feeling so much at ease with Avery. There was still a lot they had to learn about each other, but so far things were going wonderfully well and he felt optimistic about the future.

"I forgot to tell you, I did some research and I have two names for you," she said. "I'll give them to you before you leave."

Just that quickly he had murder on his mind. God, he wished something would break on the mummy murders. "Thanks, I appreciate any help I can get."

"How many men do you have on your list so far?"

"Your two names make ten. We've already given the others to Chief Thompson." He frowned. "Going back in time to try to find people stationed in the area forty years ago is more difficult than I thought it would be."

"And you're sure that one of those soldiers is the killer?"

"No, I'm not sure of anything, but there's got to be a reason those army buttons were found next to Patrice's body."

"What does Chief Thompson think about all this?" she asked.

Dallas felt the frown deepen across his forehead. "He thinks the killer from forty years ago is possibly active again." Dallas, along with his brother Forrest, had been trying to aid the overworked chief.

Archer Thompson had his hands full, not only with running the department and dealing with other crimes, but also now trying to investigate murders that were both heinous and seemingly inexplicable.

"But didn't Elliot Corgan go to prison for those murders that happened forty years ago?"

"Yeah, and then he hanged himself in his cell, and there was a lot of speculation that he might have been helped along to his death," Dallas said.

"But why after all this time would the killer start up again?"

"That is the million-dollar question," he replied drily. "All I know is I intend to keep digging into finding anyone who can potentially be put on our suspect list. But I don't want you thinking about murder right now."

"Dallas, I'm not some delicate flower," she scoffed. "I like to think of myself as a tough district attorney. Murder is a part of my world, along with drug dealing and other criminal activity."

"For the next six weeks, until you deliver, I'd like you to treat yourself like you are a delicate flower," he replied. "I want you to only think happy thoughts and translate those to our babies." It felt odd yet wonderful to say those words out loud: *our babies*.

"So noted," she said with a laugh.

For the next thirty minutes they fell into fantasy talk about the adults the babies would grow up to be. "I wouldn't mind if one of them followed my footsteps into some form of law enforcement," she said.

"That would please me, too," he agreed. "But I'll love them whatever they grow up to be."

"What if our son wants to be a ballerina?" she asked, her eyes glittering with humor.

"As long as he was happy, I'd support him," he replied.

"And what if our daughter chose to be a garbage man?"

"Then I'd learn to love garbage, too."

Avery laughed. She stood and placed her hand on her stomach. "Oh, right now it feels like they're both going to be world-class acrobats, because they are definitely turning somersaults all over the place."

She moved to stand right in front of him. "Here."

To his surprise she took his hand and placed it on her stomach.

He laughed as a new joy filled him. Was that a little elbow? Was it a tiny foot he felt kicking inside her stomach? It was amazing to feel the movements that spoke of life. Once again he was struck by the miracle of it all.

Reluctantly he drew back his hand and stood. "That's amazing. Thank you for allowing me to feel that."

She stood so close to him and her evocative scent surrounded him. Rational thought was replaced with the desire to take her in his arms and taste her lips once again. As if she could read his thoughts, she leaned slightly forward and into him.

No, a little voice whispered in the back of his head. *Don't do it. Don't go there. Following through on this moment of desire will only complicate things between you.* The voice became more insistent and he obeyed it. He took a step back from her and the moment was lost.

She cleared her throat and walked over to the small built-in desk. "Just let me get those names for you before you leave." She withdrew a piece of paper from a drawer and then wrote down the information she had for him.

"I got these from some old photos on the Camp Mabry site." She walked back and handed him the piece of paper. "There are lots more pictures and rolls to check, but I haven't had time to really dig into it."

He tucked the piece of paper in his back pocket. "Still, I appreciate whatever help we can get on this."

She frowned. "Did Lulu ever come back inside?"

"I don't know. I wasn't paying any attention."

Her frown deepened. "Lulu," she called, and stepped into the living room. She called the dog's name again as she moved down the hallway, and then returned to the kitchen.

"She's not anywhere in the house, so apparently she didn't come back in." A frown creased Avery's forehead. "She never stays out this long." She walked to the back door and opened it.

Dallas followed her outside onto her deck. "Is there a gate that might have been left open?" he asked.

"There is a gate, but there's absolutely no reason it should be open. Lulu!" she called. "Where are you, baby?"

"Are there any holes in your fence where she might have gotten out?"

"Not that I know of." She called the dog's name again and this time her voice was rife with worry.

"I'll check around in the yard," he said.

"Me, too."

Together they left the deck, both of them calling the dog's name. There were decorative bushes on the left side of the yard, and Dallas headed in that direction as Avery went to the right.

The gate was closed, so Lulu hadn't wandered out of the backyard, although it was possible she might have crawled through a hole beneath the fence.

Avery continued to shout the dog's name, her cries growing more and more frantic. Then suddenly she released a scream that raised the hairs on the nape of his neck and shot a sickening jolt through him.

"Avery!" He rushed to her as she bent down and picked up a bloody and shaking Lulu in her arms.

"Oh God, we need to get to the vet's," she said with a deep sob.

"Let's go." Dallas grabbed her by the arm as she held the dog close to her chest, the blood smearing the front of her blouse.

As they went back through the house and to his truck in the driveway, Avery continued to cry and hold the poodle close to her. "Oh, sweet baby, what happened? Hang on, Lulu, we're taking you to get help. Please hang on, baby. Hurry, Dallas. We need to get to Dr. Schell's Animal Clinic."

Dallas drove as fast as the speed limit would allow, his heart thudding an anxious rhythm. Not only was he worried about poor Lulu, he was also concerned about Avery in her sobbing despair.

Within minutes they were at Dr. Schell's, Lulu's veterinarian's office. The tall, thin doctor was standing at the receptionist's desk with a younger woman who was apparently his assistant. But as soon as he saw them, without saying a word he took the dog from Avery's arms and then disappeared with his assistant into an examining room, closing the door behind them.

Avery stood for a moment staring at the door and then collapsed into one of the plastic chairs in the waiting area, sobs ripping from the very depths of her. Dallas sat next to her. He put his arm around her shoulders and pulled her close to his side.

"It's going to be okay," he said softly. "We got her here in time. Whatever happened to her, the doctor will be able to fix her right up." He spoke with an assurance he only hoped was right. He grabbed her hand in his in an effort to offer whatever comfort he could.

"There was so much blood, Dallas. What… What could have happened to her to cause so much blood?" Avery's teary eyes held his gaze, as if he might have an answer she desperately needed to hear.

"Dr. Schell will let us know what's going on," he replied, trying to assure her.

"I sh-should have checked on her s-sooner," she said with choking breaths as her sobs began to subside. "I—I should have realized something was wrong when she didn't come right back into the house."

"You can't blame yourself for whatever happened," he protested.

Slowly, she stopped crying and simply leaned against him as they waited for the doctor to tell them what had happened. Was it possible a big dog had gotten into the yard and attacked Lulu? He couldn't see how, unless the dog was big enough to jump the fence.

Had it been some sort of a rabid animal that had gone after the small, helpless dog? She was right, there had been a lot of blood…too much blood.

The receptionist offered Avery a glass of water, but Avery declined.

The minutes seemed to tick by with an agonizingly slowness. It had been a day of incredible highs…seeing his babies on the sonogram and then feeling the life kicking in her belly. And now this. His head felt like it was spinning from the roller-coaster ride of his emotions.

He couldn't imagine how distraught Avery would be if for some reason Lulu had to be put to sleep. There was no question that she loved the little pooch.

Finally, Dr. Schell walked out. Avery jumped up from her chair and Dallas rose, as well. He grabbed her by the elbow to keep her steady, unsure what was about to happen.

Dr. Schell smiled at them and relief shuddered through Dallas. Surely the veterinarian wouldn't be smiling if something was seriously wrong with Lulu.

"She's fine," Dr. Schell assured Avery. "Physically she's completely unharmed. However, Lulu is a bit traumatized. Somebody, I'm assuming not you, shaved a stripe down her back," he said.

"But what about all the blood?" Avery asked in obvious bewilderment. "She had to have been hurt somewhere."

"It was all fake blood." Dr. Schell frowned. "It's now being sold in stores because of Halloween coming in a couple of weeks. It appears somebody played a bad joke on you. I've got Linda giving Lulu a little bath right now."

Avery sagged against Dallas's side. "Thank God she's okay."

Dallas was glad the dog was all right, but immediately his mind began to work. Who had done this and why? Somebody had to have snatched the dog from the backyard, shaved her and covered her with the fake blood, then returned her. It was all crazy and hateful. Who was responsible for this and why?

"Lulu will be out in just a few minutes. I also found this tied to her collar." He held out a small plastic bag with a piece of paper folded up inside. Avery took it from him, opened the plastic bag and pulled out the note.

"WHORE. NEXT TIME IT MIGHT BE REAL BLOOD. NEXT TIME IT MIGHT BE YOURS."

Chapter 5

A cold chill washed over Avery as she stared down at the words written on the paper. Who had done this? Who had done this to Lulu and left the horrible note for her? With trembling fingers she started to crumple the paper up, but Dallas stopped her.

"Dr. Schnell, could we have an envelope?" he asked.

"I've got one right here," the receptionist said. She held out a plain white envelope. Dallas took it from her and instructed Avery to place both the plastic bag and the note into it.

She did so with her hands still trembling, and Dallas took the envelope from her. "Danny and Chad warned me that some of Dwayne Conway's thug friends were smack-talking about wanting revenge on me. But I can't believe they did this to my dog. I can't believe anyone would do this to a little dog."

At that moment Linda walked out the back room with Lulu in her arms. "Oh Lulu, my poor little baby," Avery said, and took the shivering poodle from her.

Sure enough, just as Dr. Schell had described, a long swatch of fur was missing down Lulu's back. But thankfully, she was clean and relatively unharmed by what had been done to her.

"I know not all people ascribe to the belief that dogs have human feelings like shame, but I do," Dr. Schell said. "I wouldn't be surprised if Lulu hid once you get her home. She knows something has been done to her and she's ashamed of how she looks. I just want to warn you that for the next couple of hours she might not act normal."

"I'll just have to make sure I give her extra loving," Avery replied.

"That's what this doctor would recommend," Dr. Schell replied with a smile.

Minutes later they were back in Dallas's truck and headed to her house. "I still can't believe somebody did this. What an evil, wicked thing to do to a poor, innocent dog," she said.

"What concerns me is the threat to you that was in that note," Dallas said, his tone grim. "When were you going to tell me that Chad and Danny told you about threats made toward you?"

"I didn't take it real seriously at the time, so I didn't think it was anything to talk about."

"You should have told me right away. When we get back to the house we need to call Chief Thompson."

She frowned and cuddled Lulu more tightly against her. "I hate to bother him with this. He has enough on his plate with the mummy and other murders."

"Avery, this needs to be reported and investigated," Dallas replied firmly. "That note threatened your life."

"I know," she replied softly. It felt good for him to be so protective of her. It felt good to have somebody she trusted on her side, especially since her world was suddenly tilted upside down. There was no question she was frightened by what had happened.

"I'm definitely not going to let Lulu go outside alone anymore," she said.

"At this point I'm not sure I want *you* going outside alone," he replied, as he pulled up in her driveway. His words warmed her. She was so grateful that he cared about her and was with her through this. She was definitely shaken up by what had happened and the note.

He unbuckled his seat belt and then turned to look at her. "Avery, I don't want anything happening to you. I don't want anything happening to my babies."

Reality slammed into the fantasy that had begun

spinning in her head. He really wasn't protecting her, she had to remind herself. It was all about the babies. She got out of the truck with Lulu in her arms and together she and Dallas went inside.

She sank down on the sofa while he called Chief Thompson. Lulu had stopped shivering and seemed happy to be home. Thankfully, she didn't hide, but rather curled up on her little pink bed at the end of the sofa and promptly fell asleep.

"He should be here in just a few minutes," Dallas said as he hung up his cell phone. He sank down next to her on the sofa and she fought the impulse to once again lean into him. She shouldn't depend on him. He wasn't hers to depend on. Besides, she was a strong woman. She shouldn't need to depend on anyone.

"I've had threats against me before," she said. "I was hoping these new threats were as empty as the others had been."

"You haven't had threats against you while I've been in your life," he replied.

"They usually amount to nothing."

"We'll see what Chief Thompson thinks about this," he replied. "What happened to Lulu didn't seem like nothing." He looked down. "At least Lulu seems okay."

"I need to call tomorrow and make an appointment with her groomer so her fur can be straightened out." A cold chill danced up Avery's spine once again. The image of Lulu hiding beneath a bush, covered with what she had thought was blood, would haunt her for a very long time. "It was so awful to see her...to see that blood all over her."

To her surprise and relief, he reached out and took her hand in his. "Avery, you...*we* need to take this seriously. That note threatened your life. Hopefully, somebody can pull a print off that note and we'll know who was behind this."

"That would be nice," she agreed. "I'd love to see somebody in jail for terrorizing my dog."

"I'd like to see somebody behind bars for terrorizing you," he replied. "I haven't noticed before... do you have an alarm system here?"

"I do. It was one of the first things I had installed when I moved in here. As a single woman living alone, I thought an alarm was a necessity."

"Good. That puts my mind to rest a little bit," he replied. "From now on you need to leave the house as little as possible. When you do leave here you definitely need to watch your surroundings and be on high alert."

"Trust me, you don't have to give me a talk on safety. I've been aware of safety issues since I became a prosecutor. I've always known I could be targeted by creeps."

The doorbell rang, and Dallas jumped to his feet. "That should be Chief Thompson."

He opened the front door and welcomed him in. Despite being beyond retirement age, the lawman carried his authority in the firm set of his shoulders and the direct gaze of his eyes.

He had a good reputation at the prosecutor's office and was known as a straight shooter, although Avery couldn't help but notice he looked tired and stressed out.

Avery told him about finding Lulu in the backyard and then Dallas handed him the envelope with the note inside. Avery told him what the note said before he pulled gloves on and then opened and read it for himself.

"According to Chad and Danny at the office, Dwayne Conway's buddies have been talking about getting some sort of revenge on me for him being locked up," she said.

"I'll have a chat with Chad and Danny and see if they have any more information on these threats," Archer replied. He frowned and held up the envelope Dallas had given him. "I don't hold much hope that I can lift a fingerprint off this, but I'll give it a try. These creeps are smart enough to know to wear gloves when they're creating havoc."

"We hated to bother you with this," Avery said. "With everything else you have on your plate, you don't need anything more."

"You were right to call me. We can't have one of our prosecutors being threatened. And unfortunately, other crime doesn't stop in this town just because we're investigating the mummy murder cases," Archer replied.

"Anything new on those cases?" Dallas asked.

Archer's jaw knotted with obvious tension. "Nothing. I'm hoping, once we get the list of soldiers who were stationed around the area during the time of the original murders, that something will pop open for us. But I'm also aware that it's all a long shot."

"Avery volunteered to do some research on that, as well," Dallas said. "It doesn't help that the state of Texas has or had so many Army encampments and that records from that time period haven't all been uploaded to the internet. Still, we should get through them in the next couple of days."

Archer nodded and started for the door. "I'll keep you updated on anything I find concerning this note and whoever was responsible. In the meantime, Avery, stay alert and call me if anything else happens."

The minute the lawman left the house, Avery collapsed back on the sofa. Waves of weariness washed over her. Adrenaline had spiked through her since the moment she'd seen Lulu hiding behind the bush in the backyard. The adrenaline had remained high until now, and with it draining away she was utterly exhausted.

"Are you okay?" Dallas asked, as he sank down next to her.

"I'm fine," she assured him.

"Are you scared?"

A small laugh escaped her. "Right now I think I'm too tired to be afraid."

"Are you going to be okay here alone?" His gaze held hers intently.

"I'll be fine," she assured him. She certainly didn't expect him to spend the night with her just because she got a threatening note.

"If you're sure, then I'll get out of here and let you rest. You have to be exhausted from everything that has happened today."

"I am," she admitted. "But it was a wonderful day before we found Lulu hiding in the bushes."

"It was one of the very best days of my life," he replied. He stood and held out a hand to her. "Walk me to the door so you can set your alarm after I leave."

She grasped his hand and got to her feet. Together they went to the front door, where he turned to look at her. He reached out and gently pushed a strand of her hair away from her face. "You'll be okay?"

"I'll be just fine. I doubt if anything else comes out of this. Whoever did it, they wanted to scare me and they succeeded. I wouldn't be surprised if whoever was responsible was lurking nearby, and I'm sure they enjoyed the sound of my horrified scream."

His jaw tensed. "Set your alarm, and call me if

you just need to talk or you get frightened. Now, get some rest."

"I will," she replied. She closed and locked the door behind him and then set the alarm.

It was well past dinnertime, but she wasn't a bit hungry, even though it felt as if it had been days… months ago that they'd eaten ice cream together and everything had seemed so absolutely wonderful.

"Ready for bed, Lulu?"

The poodle got out of the bed at the end of the sofa. She yawned and then gazed at Avery with soulful brown eyes. Avery bent down and picked the dog up in her arms.

"Don't worry, baby. I won't let anyone hurt you ever again, and tomorrow, hopefully, Regina can straighten out your fur for you." She carried the dog back to her bedroom and then set her on the floor.

She was tempted to let Lulu sleep in her bed, but that had been something she'd never allowed. Thankfully, Lulu ran to the doggie bed, curled up and yawned once again. Avery was glad the little dog didn't seem to suffer any lingering effects from what had happened to her.

Avery changed from her street clothes into a short maternity nightshirt. She then went into the bathroom and washed her face and brushed her teeth. Finally, she closed her bedroom door so Lulu couldn't leave the room in the middle of the night to use the doggie door.

She found an old newspaper in her closet and unfolded it and placed it on the floor in front of the bedroom door, just in case Lulu couldn't wait to do her business until morning, and then Avery got into bed.

As tired as she was, that didn't stop the events of the day from whirling around in her head. She'd been so terrified when she'd seen Lulu. All that blood… A shiver shook through her and she pulled the blankets more closely around her.

Evil. It had been such an evil, terrible thing for somebody to do. Who even thought about doing something so heinous? Whoever was responsible for this was definitely sick and evil.

Was she frightened about the threat that had been made toward her? Maybe a little, but not overly so. She'd told Dallas the truth when she'd said she'd had other threats directed at her before, and nothing had ever come of them. Hopefully, whoever did this was done.

Still, she definitely intended to watch her back whenever she left the house.

She released a long, deep sigh, and just that quickly her mind went from unknown threats to Dallas. Before Lulu had disappeared it had been a magical day.

Watching his facial features expressing awe and joy while he saw the sonogram had warmed her heart in a way it had never been before. Then when he'd felt the babies kicking and moving around in her belly she'd experienced the tremendous joy of more intimately sharing the miracle of life.

But before he'd stepped away from her there had been a moment when she'd thought he was going to kiss her. That moment was emblazoned in her mind, because she'd wanted him to. She'd desperately wanted him to kiss her.

And that was definitely dangerous. She had to remember that he was with her now only because she was carrying his children. She had to remind herself that if he worried about her safety, if he felt a certain closeness with her, it was all because in a month and a half she would give birth to his babies.

Even knowing that, she really wished he would have kissed her.

Dallas sank down in his recliner, his brain spinning with concerns for Avery. What had happened to her dog, along with the note around Lulu's neck, had shaken him up far more than he had shown her.

He wanted to put her in a protective plastic bubble to make sure no harm came to her and the babies. What kind of a person threatened a pregnant woman? The lowest of the low, he thought darkly. And who did something like that to a poor, helpless little dog? Who was this person or people?

Hopefully, this was the end of it and nothing more would happen. Hopefully, Avery was right when she said the threats never escalated into anything else and remained just empty intimidations.

A knock sounded on his door and he jumped up to answer. "Hey, brother," he said to Forrest, stepping back so he could enter. "Want something to drink?"

"No, thanks, I'm good," Forrest replied, as he eased down on the sofa. "I just haven't seen or heard from you in the last few days so I figured I'd stop by and make sure you were still alive and kicking."

Dallas laughed and sank back down in his recliner. "I'm still alive, but I have been busy."

"So, what's going on? I know you haven't been working with the other men on the storm damage." Forrest eyed him curiously.

Until this moment Dallas hadn't told any of his family about Avery. Everything with her had happened so fast and he just hadn't had time to tell anyone. "You know Avery Logan, right?"

"Of course. She's one of us good guys. I'm hoping once we catch the creep responsible for the murders, she'll be the prosecutor to put him behind bars for good," Forrest replied.

Forrest had been a respected detective in Austin before a bullet in his leg had ended his career. He had received special dispensation to get his badge back and work on the mummy murders here in Whisperwood.

"Did you know she was carrying twins?" Dallas asked.

"I think I might have heard that." Forrest frowned at him curiously. "Why? What's all the interest in Avery?"

"Well, they're mine, that's why. Avery is carrying my babies."

Forrest straightened up and stared at him as if he'd just sprouted a horn, announced he was marrying his horse and riding off into the sunset. "Is this some kind of a joke? You never mentioned before that you were dating Avery."

"I never mentioned dating her because I didn't date her." He looked at his brother sheepishly. "The twins are the result of a one-night stand."

Forrest continued to stare at him. "A one-night stand without any birth control? Whoa, brother."

"Definitely my bad," Dallas agreed.

"So, when did this one-night stand happen?"

"About seven and a half months ago, when I was here on leave for a few days. You may remember I wasn't in a very good place during that visit." Dallas knew his brother would recall his deep grief over his wife's death when he'd come home for that visit. "Avery and I bumped into each other in the bar."

"You obviously did more than just bump into her," Forrest said drily.

Dallas laughed. "Yeah, well, that night one thing led to another, and the main thing is I'm going to be a father, Forrest." Dallas couldn't help the swell of joy that filled his voice and the excitement he felt at sharing the news with his brother.

"You sound happy about this."

"I am. I've never been so happy in my life."

Forrest grinned at him. "Then congratulations, brother. So, are you and Avery together now?"

"No, although we're spending a lot of time together to get to know each other better. There's nothing romantic going on there, but it's important we're both on the same page for the sake of our babies."

Dallas was aware that his words were a bit of a little white lie. He did feel something, a faint whisper of a romantic pull toward Avery, but he was confused by his own feelings for her. In any case he had no intention of following through on any kind of romantic emotions where she was concerned. Anything like that was just asking for trouble.

"Have you told Mom and Dad?" Forrest asked.

"No, not yet."

"Why not?"

"I only found out myself that day I went with you to the courthouse. It's taken me the last several days to process the news myself. Tell me, what's it like to be a father?" Forrest had become an instant father when he'd fallen in love with Rae Lemmon, who had a two-month-old son.

Forrest smiled. "It's awesome. I never dreamed I could love anyone like I love Rae and little Connor. When Connor smiles at me I feel like I'm on top of the world. I love being a father and I know you're going to love it, too."

"I already love it and the twins aren't even here yet." He told Forrest about going to the doctor's office and getting to hear and see his babies.

"And I suppose you have their picture hanging on your refrigerator," Forrest said.

"I do," Dallas replied with a laugh.

"Yeah, well, you'd better tell Mom and Dad before they hear it from somebody else. Mom will be so excited about it. You know how she is about grandchildren."

"I know. I'll tell them tomorrow. Now, on another note, is there any more news about the mummy killings or Patrice Eccleston's murder?" Even though Dallas had asked Chief Thompson the same question, he knew the chief might not have been so forthcoming, since he had been at Avery's house on another matter.

Forrest frowned. "Right now the investigation seems to be stalled out. It would help if the army records from forty years ago were all in one place and uploaded to files that we could easily access."

"Speaking of that…" Dallas stood and pulled out the piece of paper with the two names Avery had written down. "Avery volunteered to help us and she found two men who had been stationed in the area. She intends to continue to search, but she has her own issue going on right now." He handed the note to his brother.

"Issue? You mean her pregnancy?"

"That and the fact that somebody has threatened her life." Dallas went on to explain to Forrest about what had happened that day with Lulu, and the note that had been tied around the little dog's neck.

"Wow, that's tough. And she thinks it's because she was successful in putting away Dwayne Conway?"

"That's the thought," he replied. "A couple of her coworkers told her some of Conway's friends were talking smack about wanting revenge."

"And what are you going to do about it?" Forrest asked.

"Right now I'm hoping it was a one-time desire to terrorize her and whoever did it is done with her."

"And if they aren't done?"

"I'll do whatever needs to be done to protect her and those babies," Dallas replied fervently.

Forrest grinned at him. "I wouldn't expect anything different from you. We Colton boys always protect those we love."

Forrest had certainly protected Rae and little Connor when one of the mummified bodies had been found in Rae's backyard and threats had been made against her.

The two brothers visited for a little while longer and then Forrest left. Dallas settled back in his chair and released a weary sigh.

Once again he thought of that moment when he'd wanted to kiss Avery. Maybe he was spending too much time with her. He should have just taken her to her doctor appointment and then taken her back home instead of prolonging their day together with the ice cream and then coffee at her house.

But then he wouldn't have been there when she found Lulu. She would have been all alone in her terror. And now with the threat made against her, he didn't feel as if it was the time to pull back from her. At least she had a home security system, which somewhat put his mind at ease.

Maybe a good night's sleep would straighten out his emotions where Avery was concerned. And in the morning he'd join the other men for some work. There was nothing better to clear his head than being on the back on a horse with the sunshine on his shoulders.

With his plans made for the next morning, he decided to call it a night. Before he went into his own bedroom, he stood in the threshold of the nursery.

The sight of the two cribs filled him with a tremendous joy. *Ivy.* Her name jumped into his mind and some of the joy diminished as a familiar edge of grief whispered through him.

This was what they had planned together. Not necessarily twins, but they had definitely dreamed about the day they would become parents. They had talked about it often…about buying a house and having a child or two. They hadn't been able to wait to start their life together. But her last tour of duty had ended all that.

He'd had his one true love and he would never, ever love another woman like he had Ivy. She was in his heart forever and there just wasn't room for another love like that. There would never be room for another woman in his heart.

He would coparent with Avery and together they would share the joy of loving the twins. His desire to kiss her had been nothing more than a crazy reaction to feeling the life in her stomach.

Turning away from the nursery, he already felt more centered. Through a wild twist of fate, Avery was the mother of his children. He would support her and be there for her through the last of her pregnancy. But once the twins were a little bit older he would only see Avery when he picked up and brought back the children on his parental visits.

She was the mother of his children, and that's all she would ever be in his life.

Chapter 6

Avery awoke early the next morning and immediately called her groomer, Regina McGraw, to see if she could fit Lulu into her schedule sometime that day.

"Sorry, Avery, I can't get her in today. I'm totally booked. It will have to be tomorrow about eleven," Regina replied. "I apologize, but I'm really full up today."

"That's okay. Tomorrow will be fine," Avery said, hiding her disappointment. She'd hoped to get Lulu cut so that she wouldn't have to see her poor baby with the swatch of missing fur and be reminded of that moment when she'd found her under the bush.

Still, after all the drama of the day before, a day

inside the house doing a whole lot of nothing sounded just fine to her. And that's exactly what she did. The only time she poked her head outside was when Lulu went out to do her business. Each time that happened she made sure her senses were on high alert for anyone lurking around her backyard.

She ate a leisurely breakfast and then worked on the computer until noon. She had just finished lunch when Dallas called.

"Just thought I'd check in to see how you're doing today," he said.

"I'm doing fine," she replied. "Lulu and I are just having a nice, quiet day." She tried not to focus on the warmth the mere sound of his voice shot through her.

"That's good," he replied. "I'm sure you needed a quiet day after yesterday. I just wanted to check in to make sure you were doing all right."

"I just finished lunch. What are you doing today?"

"I've been working with some of the other cowboys this morning on more storm cleanup. Right now I'm on my horse and headed back to my cabin for some lunch. Do you have any plans for the afternoon?"

"Right now my plan is a nice, long nap," she replied.

"Then I'll let you get to it and I'll talk to you later," he replied.

After they hung up she curled up on the sofa.

She'd thought about inviting Dallas to dinner that evening but had stopped herself. He needed to have his own life without them being together every single day. Even the very best of friends didn't see each other all the time.

The rest of the day passed quietly, and the next morning at ten forty she loaded Lulu into the car for her grooming appointment.

Regina was a popular groomer and kept super busy, with tons of clients in town. Her business was in an addition that had been built onto her home on the outskirts of town.

It was a beautiful day with the sun shining brightly. Despite everything that was happening in her life, Avery had slept like a baby last night. She'd feared she'd suffer nightmares, but thankfully, she hadn't.

She rolled down her window to enjoy the crisp, fresh air. As she passed the turnoff to the Colton ranch, she wondered what Dallas was doing this morning. Then she reminded herself that it was really none of her business. She had to stop wondering what he was doing when he wasn't with her. She had to stop even thinking about him when they weren't together.

It was another ten miles to Regina's place, and that stretch held nothing but fencing and pastureland on either side of the two-lane road.

Regina lived on ten acres that were mostly devoted to her love of animals. There were several horses in a corral, goats in a pen and dog runs for canines of all shapes and sizes.

Her home was a small ranch, but the addition that had been built on for her business was almost as big as the house itself. While the house itself was white, the addition was a bright pink, with dogs and cats of all colors and sizes painted on the walls.

Avery parked in front and left the car with Lulu in her arms. A bell tinkled when she walked in the door to a small reception area. There was a desk behind a long counter, but Avery had never seen anyone seated there in all the times she'd been here.

She waited only a minute or so before Regina appeared from the back room. Avery quickly explained what had happened to the dog.

"Ah, let me get a look at that poor baby," she said as she took Lulu from Avery's arms. "Somebody should be shot for doing this."

"I completely agree," Avery replied.

Regina's plump fingers raked through Lulu's fur. When she looked back at Avery her bright blue eyes sparkled. "This isn't going to be a problem. With my clipper and scissors I can turn her back into the diva she is."

Avery laughed. "I knew you could."

"I've got several dogs back there. Why don't you give me until about four this afternoon? I should have her ready by then."

"That's fine with me. So, I'll see you around four."

Avery watched as the heavyset woman disappeared with Lulu into the back, and then she turned and left the building.

Lulu never minded coming here. Regina made sure the last thing she did before handing a dog back to its owner was give it a spoonful of peanut butter. That way the dog's last memory of being at the groomer was getting to eat a delicious goodie.

Avery pulled back out on the road that would take her home, and had been driving only a minute or two when she saw a pickup in her rearview mirror. The vehicle was advancing on her fairly quickly.

"You're obviously speeding, buddy," she muttered. She fought the impulse to step on the gas. She was going the speed limit and refused to go faster. The coast was clear for him or her to just go around her.

When she looked in her rearview mirror once again, the truck was right on her butt. It was a dark blue or black truck with tinted windows that made it impossible for her to see who was driving. All she knew for certain was the vehicle was riding way too close to her for comfort.

She moved over as far as she could in the lane to make it easy for the truck to go around her, but instead of doing so it smashed into her. The force of the collision ripped the steering wheel right out of her hands. She gasped and grappled with it in an effort to regain control before she flew off the pavement and into the nearby ditch.

What was wrong with the person driving? Was he or she drunk? Drug impaired? Had the truck accidentally hit her? What in the hell was going on? As her seat belt seemed to tighten around her belly, she thought of her babies.

She yelled as the truck banged into her car again. It was definitely no accident. Panic fluttered in her heart and seared through her veins. She stepped on the gas in an effort to escape the other vehicle.

"What are you doing?" she screamed. All she could think about were the babies she carried. She couldn't be involved in a wreck. She had to maintain control of her car for her twins' sake.

Despite her effort to outrun the truck it crashed into her again. Her car careened to the right, nearly sliding into the ditch before she managed to straighten it.

She felt as if she was in a horror film, with a killer truck chasing her down a deserted road. And why was there nobody else on the road to see what was happening? What *was* happening? What did the driver of the truck hope to do? Drive her off into the ditch and then what? Shoot her? Kill her?

As she remembered the note that had been tied around Lulu's neck, her fear exploded. Sobs choked her and terrified tears half blurred her vision. Ahead she saw the turnoff for the Colton ranch. If she took it would the truck continue to follow her?

Praying that the answer was no, she slowed at the very last possible minute and then yanked the wheel to make the turn. Dust billowed up behind her, but thankfully, the truck shot on past the turn.

Still, she drove as fast as possible toward Dallas's cabin. She had no idea if the truck that had followed her, the driver who had attacked her, would turn around and come after her. She grabbed her cell phone out of her purse but was too busy frantically driving to make a call.

Fear clawed at her throat as her eyes shot to her rearview mirror over and over again. She didn't see anyone following her, but feared the truck would suddenly appear right behind her once again.

She finally pulled up in front of Dallas's cabin and skidded to a halt next to his truck. *Safety.* She continued to sob as she grabbed her phone and raced for his front door.

"Dallas!" She beat on the door with her fist. Fear was still a frantic, screaming beast inside her. There was no answer. She banged on the door once again. "Dallas, please help me."

Despite the presence of his truck in front of the cabin, apparently he wasn't home. Oh God, if the guy in the truck returned, she would be a sitting target standing here. Through her tears she frantically looked around. She finally crouched behind an evergreen bush on the left side of the porch.

With trembling fingers, and trying to staunch her tears, she punched in Dallas's number. He answered on the first ring.

"Dallas, I'm—I'm at your cabin. Could…could you please come home?"

"Avery, what's wrong?"

"Please, come home. I—I just need you."

"Sit tight. I'll be right there."

She clenched the phone tightly in her trembling hand and tried to control the terror that still iced the insides of her body. If the truck had come after her, surely it would have appeared by now. Even knowing that logically, she couldn't stop the waves of fear that continued to wash over her.

She didn't know how long she'd been behind the bush when Dallas appeared. He was on horseback and riding hard and fast toward the cabin. He looked like the hero in a Western movie riding to the heroine's rescue.

He pulled up and dismounted, and she stood up from behind the bush. "Avery!"

Instantly she began to cry again. He rushed over to her, took her by the shoulders and gazed at her worriedly. "Are you okay?"

She nodded. "I—I am now."

"What happened? What's going on?"

She nervously looked at the road. "Please, can… can we go inside?"

"Of course." He took her by the arm and led her to the door. He unlocked it and they went inside. He guided her to the sofa and then took her hands in his. "Now, tell me what has you so upset."

She told him about the truck slamming into her car over and over again, and Dallas's frown deepened with every word she spoke. "Did you get the make or model of the truck?" he asked when she was finished.

"No, I only know it was either a black or a very dark blue pickup."

"Could you tell who was driving?"

"No," she replied. "I can't even tell you if the driver was male or female. The windows were tinted. I was so terrified, Dallas. I was afraid my body would be found in a ditch on the side of the road."

He pulled her into his arms and she cried once again, though this time they were tears of relief because she knew she was safe. She finally stopped crying and he released her.

"We need to call Chief Thompson." He got up off the sofa.

She remained seated and listened as he made the phone call. When he had finished telling the chief what had happened, he hung up. "He wants us to drive your car to the station. Are you okay to drive? I'll follow you into town."

She released a tremulous breath. "I can drive." She started to rise.

"Sit tight and relax for a few minutes. I'm not ready to leave yet. Do you want anything? A glass of water…a cup of hot tea?"

"No, thanks," she replied. Now that the abject fear

had gone away, she felt both exhausted and slightly nauseous.

"I'll just be in my room for a few minutes," he said.

She waved her hand at him. "Take care of whatever you need to. I just appreciate everything you're doing."

"And I'm glad you had the foresight to come here when you were being chased."

"Me, too." She leaned back and closed her eyes as Dallas disappeared into his bedroom.

The note she had received the day before, tied around Lulu's neck, had apparently been a very real threat. Somebody wanted her either badly hurt or dead. But who?

Dwayne Conway had a bunch of thug friends. Who among them was behind this? She had had moments of being afraid for herself before, but nothing in the slightest compared to this.

She moved her hands to her stomach and rubbed it slowly…lovingly. She would have died if something had happened to her twins.

What she was now afraid of was that somebody would kill her before she gave birth to her beautiful babies. She didn't care so much about herself, but her children had to live.

Questions once again burned in her brain. Who had been driving that truck? What had the plan really been—to run her off the road to scare her? Or had it truly been a plan for murder?

And more frightening, what might come next?

Would another attempt be made on her life? If so, then when? And where? There was no way for her to know what to expect.

"All set," Dallas said, as he walked back into the room with a large duffel bag in his hand.

She stood and eyed it. "Are you planning on leaving town?"

"No. I'm staying in town. In fact, I'm moving in with you, Avery."

She stared at him in stunned surprise. Moving in? "Dallas," she began to protest.

He held up a hand to halt anything she might be going to say. "I won't argue with you about this, Avery. You have not only been verbally threatened, but somebody just tried to run you off the road. Somebody wants to hurt you, and until we know who that somebody is, from now on I intend to be with you day and night."

Tears threatened to fall once again as Avery left the cabin with Dallas by her side. She didn't know if she was emotional because she felt as if her life had suddenly spiraled completely out of control, or because she was eternally grateful that at least for now, Dallas was going to be her personal bodyguard.

They dropped Avery's car off at the police station, where, hopefully, techs could pull some paint off her smashed rear bumper and back end that would point to a specific make and model of the attacking truck.

Once they were finished making a detailed report, they went to her house. The minute they walked inside a line of worry creased her forehead.

"What's wrong?" he asked, and set his duffel bag down.

"I have a home office set up in my spare bedroom and the nursery in the other spare room. I don't have a bedroom for you to sleep in."

"Don't worry about that. The sofa is just fine with me," he assured her.

"You won't be comfortable there," she protested.

He smiled at her. "Avery, I was in the army. I've slept on rocky inclines and in dark, dank holes in the ground. Trust me, I'll be just fine on your sofa."

The line in her forehead smoothed. "Can I get you something? Maybe a cup of coffee?"

"I never turn down the offer of coffee." They moved into the kitchen, where he sat at the table and watched as she got the coffee ready.

When he thought of how she had looked, bent down and hiding behind the bush next to his cabin, he wanted to hurt somebody. As he'd held her and felt her trembling with terror, he'd wanted to kill somebody.

Who was responsible for what was happening to her? Would they have killed Avery if they had managed to force her off the road? God, the very idea chilled him. It would have been a triple murder, for his babies would have probably died along with their mother.

He suddenly remembered the thug who had bumped into Avery at the diner. At the time it had seemed like it could have been an accident, but was he the one behind these threats?

"What was the name of that guy who bumped into you at the diner the other night?" he asked, as she set the cup of coffee before him.

"Joel Asman. Why?" She sat across from him.

"Do you know the names of some of Dwayne Conway's other cohorts?"

She frowned once again. "There's Phil Saunders and Ray McMann and Chuck Owens. I only know them because I've had a few run-ins with each of them in court. But I know there are others. Why? Do you intend to take them out one by one and beat them up in an alley?"

He didn't miss her attempt to try to interject some humor in the situation. "Hell, no. Forget about taking them out one by one. I'd take them all out there together and still beat their butts." He was grateful to see a sparkle in her eyes that hadn't been there since she'd shown up at his cabin.

However, there was nothing funny about what had happened to her, and the sparkle in her eyes lasted for only a moment. "Unfortunately, we can't be sure it's one of those men. Like I said before, there are a lot of thugs and dangerous dope dealers in town," she murmured.

She suddenly slapped her hands down on the tabletop. "I hate drug dealers. They are the absolute scum of the earth and they help people destroy themselves. They thrive while other people die."

He sat back in his chair and looked at her in surprise. Her outburst had come out of nowhere, but tears were welling up in her eyes. Then he thought he knew what was going on with her. "Who did you know who died?" he asked softly.

"Nobody in particular," she answered quickly, but the tears began to ooze down her cheeks.

He reached across the table and took one of her hands in his. "Talk to me, Avery. Why are you crying?"

She hesitated a moment and then squeezed his hand tightly. "My brother, Zeke. His real name was Ezekiel, but that was too big a name for a little boy, and so he was Zeke. And he died a little over a year ago from a heroin overdose." She pulled her hand from Dallas's, got up from the table and left the kitchen.

He waited a moment and then went in search of her. He didn't have to look far. She stood in the living room, in front of the windows that faced the backyard.

He walked up behind her, but before he reached her she whirled around to face him and quickly swept tears from her cheeks. "I'm sorry," she said, her voice still shaky with emotion.

"Don't be."

She walked over to the sofa and sank down. He sat next to her. "You want to talk about it?"

She sighed. "Unfortunately, it's an all-too-common story. Zeke always struggled a bit with depression. I think part of it had to do with the fact that our father was a mostly absent force in our lives. Oh, he meant well, but he'd work all day and then in the evenings he'd either go to the bar to hang out with his buddies or he'd date. He dated a lot after my mother died."

"How old were you when you lost your mother?"

"I was ten and Zeke was seven. I was kind of like his mom while we grew up. I knew when he was about eighteen he started dabbling in drugs, mostly smoking marijuana and partying a lot. I lectured him about the drug use, that not only was it illegal, but it was also bad for him."

She sighed again. "Despite my lecturing him, by the time he was twenty it was more than just dabbling and more than just weed. Then he got his job at Sanders's Animal Farm and he was thrilled. Zeke loved animals of all kinds, and a place where animals were not only lodged, but also bred was a perfect fit for him."

She paused and rubbed large circles on her stomach, as if she found the motion soothing. "And that job remained a good fit for him until he was about twenty-seven. Still, I occasionally wondered if he was using." She moved her hand from her stomach to her forehead and rubbed it back and forth, as if her memories had created a bad headache.

"Zeke and I checked in with each other every day without fail. Suddenly he wasn't calling me as often, and my calls to him often went unanswered." She dropped her hand back to her lap. "When I finally confronted him he admitted he was shooting heroin. He'd lost his job, he didn't have money to pay his next month's rent and he had no food."

She fell silent for a long moment, obviously lost in painful memories as tears once again filled her eyes. "I tried everything to save him. I begged him to go to rehab and I'd pay for it. I paid his rent and bought him food. When he wasn't at home I drove the streets to find him. I went to Al-Anon meetings and learned I was enabling him. So I tried to do things differently. He made me so many promises, and each time he did, I believed him. But those promises were always broken."

She looked at Dallas, and in the depths of her eyes he saw such pain it almost gutted him. "Then one morning I went over to check on him and he was dead on the floor in his bedroom. My little brother was dead, Dallas."

As she began to weep in earnest, he wrapped her in his arms and held her tightly. Oh, he knew her pain. He understood her grief. The agony of death was no stranger to either one of them. Somehow knowing that she had suffered such a loss made him feel closer to her.

"I'm sorry, Avery. I'm so sorry for your loss." He rubbed his hands up and down her back, wishing he had a magic elixir to stop her grief.

She cried for only a minute or two and then stopped and moved out of his arms. She raised her head to look at him and once again he felt the desire to kiss her...to steal the grief from her by covering her mouth with his.

Her lips, so intimately close, trembled slightly, as if with her own need of him. Oh, sweet Jesus, but he wanted to kiss her. And it had nothing to do with shared grief, but rather hot desire.

She snapped up and out of his arms, her gaze flitting away from his as her cheeks turned a blushing pink. "I'm sorry. The grief, it sometimes creeps up on me. That night when we met in the bar, it was the one-month anniversary of Zeke's death. I was feeling wild and reckless and that's why I went to the motel with you."

"I know grief sometimes makes people do crazy things." He pulled his mind away from desire and back to the conversation. It was interesting that he'd been feeling those same kinds of things when he'd gone to the bar. He'd been mourning the death of Ivy, who, on that night, had been gone for three months.

"The worst part is the heroin Zeke used that morning had been laced liberally with fentanyl. Some dope dealer decided to cut his heroin with a drug that kills, just to make more crap to sell."

"And that's why you hate drug dealers."

She nodded. "Of course, ultimately it was Zeke who took the dope, and I'm still angry with him for choosing the path he did. I just know there are families who struggle with an addict. There are mothers and fathers who go to bed at night fearing the death of the addict. They wonder if they've done too much or too little to help the person get clean. I really hate that there are too many drugs being sold on the streets and in alleys in Whisperwood. And now, enough of this."

She stood. "I didn't even give you a chance to drink your coffee. Come back to the kitchen and I'll make you a fresh cup."

While he drank a new cup of coffee the conversation remained light, despite the many troubling concerns he had, and he knew she must be entertaining, as well.

All he could do right now was make sure he was by her side no matter where she went or what she did. They had reported the incident to Chief Thompson and left Avery's car at the station. Now there was nothing more they could do but be on guard for the next attack that would happen.

And the terrifying thing was, he had a gut certainty that another one would.

Chapter 7

At four thirty they left the house to go pick up Lulu. When they reached the stretch of road where the truck had banged into the back end of her car, distress and anxiety pressed tight in Avery's chest as she remembered how terrified she had been.

Who had been in that truck? Who had tried to wreck her car and force her off the road? She shuddered as she thought of what might have happened if she'd lost control of her vehicle.

"Avery, we aren't being followed," Dallas assured her the fourth time she twisted to look out the back window. "Try to relax. All that stress you're carrying can't be good for the babies."

She settled back in her seat and released several

deep, cleansing breaths, knowing he was right. No matter what was happening in her life, she needed to think of the health of her twins. She just hoped Chief Thompson would have some answers for them about the driver who had attacked her.

She breathed a sigh of relief when they pulled up in front of Regina's. The bell tinkled over the doorway as they walked in. It was only a minute before Regina appeared from her back room.

She looked at Dallas in surprise. "If it isn't Dallas Colton. Hey, Dallas, it's been a while."

"Hi, Regina. It's been a lot of years," he agreed.

"Ah, but I'd recognize that handsome mug of yours no matter how many years passed," Regina said, and then looked around as if in mock fear. "Better not let Joe hear me talking to another man like that. He'd quit making his special pulled pork for me."

Both Avery and Dallas laughed. Regina and Joe McGraw had been married for more years than Avery had been alive. It had always been obvious to others that the two of them adored each other.

She then smiled at Avery. "When Dallas was a young pup, he used to bring in stray dogs he found and have them washed and groomed."

"That's nice," Avery replied, and looked at him with a new respect. Him being kind to animals, especially strays, only assured her once again that he was going to be a loving, caring father.

"Was Lulu good for you?" she asked.

Regina smiled. "That sweet baby is always good for me. She doesn't have an aggressive bone in her body. Let me go get her for you."

She disappeared into the back once again and Avery looked at Dallas. "Strays, huh?"

He shrugged. "I'd occasionally run across strays and they were usually filthy and matted. Once they were cleaned up I'd try to find a good home for them. It was no big deal."

At that moment Regina returned with Lulu in her arms. The dog had been shaved except for cute poodle puffs around her ankles. She sported little pink bows at her ears and matching pink polish on her nails. "Oh, Regina, she looks so cute," Avery said as she took Lulu from the groomer's arms. "You'll bill me?"

Regina laughed. "You know I will."

Minutes later they were in the car and headed back to Avery's house, and for the first time she began to process the fact that Dallas would not be going to his cabin that night.

"Uh, I didn't know you would be at my place this evening so I didn't pull anything out of the freezer to cook for dinner," she said.

"Don't stress, I'll just order a pizza." He flashed her a quick glance. "Avery, I don't want you stressing about anything. I don't expect you to cook for me every night. You don't have to worry about picking up after me or entertaining me. The main thing is I'm not going to let anyone hurt you. You're safe with me."

She hadn't realized how tense, how filled with anxiety she had been until some of those emotions drifted away with the determination she heard in his words.

Other than that it was a quiet ride home, and once they were inside the house he got on the phone to order the pizza. When he was finished she gestured to his duffel bag.

"Feel free to hang your clothes in the spare room closet, and you can put your toiletries in the guest bathroom. I have a bathroom off my bedroom that I use."

"I'll take care of that right now."

While he unpacked, she sank down on the sofa with Lulu in her lap. The day had been exhausting. From the horrifying car drive that morning to Dallas moving in, she felt overwhelmed with everything.

There was no question she was grateful Dallas was here with her, because there was no question that whoever wanted to harm her might not be finished trying to achieve that goal. A chill worked through her at that thought.

Hopefully, despite everything else he had on his plate, Chief Thompson and his men could figure out who was behind these threats and get them arrested.

"All done," Dallas said, as he came back into the living room. Lulu jumped down from her lap and headed for the doggie door. Avery started to get up, but Dallas waved her back down. "Sit tight. I'll go out with her." He opened the back door and disappeared.

Avery got up from the sofa and went into the pantry. On the floor, tucked back in a corner, were doggie training pads. She'd used them when she'd first been training Lulu, and now she was going to use them again.

There was no way she wanted Lulu to go outside by herself, so she intended to throw the metal pins that would stop the dog door from opening. At least during the night she'd keep the door locked and put down a puppy pad.

There were several habits that were going to have to be broken for now. She could no longer walk into the kitchen first thing in the morning in her bra and panties to make a cup of tea. Not that she'd done that recently, but occasionally that's the way she started the day.

No longer could she just jump into the car and drive to the grocery store for a gallon of milk or a loaf of bread. Thought and planning would have to be in her mind at all times.

And how long would this nightmare go on? How long would Dallas be willing to put his life on hold to be her personal bodyguard? She'd already been terrorized twice. Was the person—or people—behind it done now? And even if they were, how would she and Dallas know that?

He and Lulu came back into the house and Dallas locked the door after them. She told him her plan about the doggie door. "It will just be for the nights, when we aren't available to go out with her."

"Sounds like a good plan to me," he agreed. At that moment the doorbell rang. "That must be our pizza."

Avery stifled a gasp as he pulled a gun from the back of his waistband. She hadn't noticed the weapon before. He answered the door and then placed his weapon on the nearby coffee table so he could pay and grab the pizza.

Once he'd done that he carried his gun and the pizza into the kitchen. He set the gun on a nearby countertop and the pizza box in the center of the table.

"Do you have paper plates?"

"In the pantry. I'll grab them." She got the plates and then the two of them sat to eat, while Lulu enjoyed a chew bone.

"What do you think about Fred and Wilma?" he asked, as he served her a piece of the pepperoni pie.

She laughed and shook her head. "No way. You are not naming the twins after prehistoric cartoon characters."

"Then I guess Tweety and Sylvester is out, too."

"You're just trying to make me laugh," she said accusingly.

He grinned at her. "I like the sound of your laughter."

"Thanks. I find yours pleasant, too." She picked off a piece of pepperoni and popped it into her mouth. "I'll try not to drive you crazy while you're here."

He looked at her curiously. "How would you make me crazy?"

"Sometimes I get up in the middle of the night because I can't get comfortable and my back hurts."

"That won't make me crazy," he replied easily.

"And sometimes I leave my breakfast dishes in the sink until lunch."

"Still not crazy." He smiled at her once again. "Avery, I'm a pretty laid-back guy. It would take a lot for you to drive me crazy."

"We'll see about that," she replied, with a smile of her own.

As they ate they somehow got on the topic of pets they'd had in their past. "We always had dogs when I was growing up," he said.

"Zeke was always bringing home animals. Dogs… cats…he even adopted a pet toad that lived under a rock in our backyard. I think he was about six at the time." She smiled sadly. "He was such a gentle man, but he was tortured with demons for most of his life."

"I'll bet you were a great big sister."

"I certainly tried to be."

Dallas gazed at her warmly. "You're going to be a terrific mother."

"I intend to be," she replied firmly. "It's probably

going to be challenging with twins, but I'm more than up for the challenge."

"And I'll be right at your side, helping you out," he replied.

"I really appreciate you being here with me now, Dallas," she said. "I'll admit I'm a little scared, although what I'm hoping is that after terrorizing me this morning, the attacks are done."

He stared at her for a long moment and any warmth she might have felt wafting from him disappeared. His jaw set and a knot began to pulse there. His mouth became a thin slash.

"Unfortunately, I don't have that same hope. What they did to Lulu was terrorizing. What they did this morning was more. As far as I'm concerned it was attempted murder, and I don't think they're done yet. I fear that they're just getting started."

He shouldn't have said it. The minute the words left his mouth she paled, and he instantly wished he could take the words back. "Avery, I'm so sorry. I shouldn't have said that."

"No, I want to know what you're thinking. I always want to know what you're thinking." The natural color began to fill her cheeks once again.

"But the good news is we know somebody wants to harm you and we can be prepared and be on alert. I've told you before and I'll tell you again, as long as there is breath in my body nobody is going to hurt you."

"And on that note, I'm eating another piece of pizza." She pulled another slice from the box to her plate. "Thankfully, talk of my own demise does nothing to diminish my appetite," she said wryly.

They finished the meal, cleaned up the kitchen and then went into the living room to numb out in front of the television.

He could tell she was relaxing by her slow and even breathing and how she stroked her stomach in small circles. Good. He wanted her relaxed. She'd been far too stressed for the past couple days.

The television show playing was a silly sitcom and it warmed his heart each time she laughed. It was the perfect way to end the night, with her relaxed and laughing.

It was just after eight when she got up from the sofa. "I think I'll call it a night." She frowned. "Are you sure you're going to be okay on the sofa?"

"I'll be just fine," he assured her, and stood, as well.

"I'll bring you a pillow and blanket." She left the room and returned a few minutes later with the items. "Then I guess I'll just say good-night."

"Good night, Avery. I hope you have sweet dreams."

He watched her go down the hall and heard the soft sound of her bedroom door closing. He sat back down on the sofa and turned off the television.

He needed to listen to the normal sounds of the house and become familiar with them so he didn't jump and grab his gun a hundred times during the night.

The sound of the furnace whooshing on and off and the faint hum of the refrigerator were a normal conversation happening in the house. They created a white noise that he would easily be able to dismiss.

At least the alarm was set, so he would be alerted if anyone tried to break in. However, he didn't know if the alarm included all the windows. He should have asked Avery about that. He'd have to ask her tomorrow.

He made a quick call to his brother Forrest, to let him know what was happening and that Dallas would be at Avery's place for an undetermined amount of time. He also made a call to his brother Donovan, to keep him up to date with what was going on.

He'd brought his computer with him, so while he was here he could continue to look for the names of army men who had been in the area forty years before.

Despite everything that had happened to Avery over the past two days, Dallas hadn't forgotten that a serial killer was working in Whisperwood, a killer he wanted to help get off the streets.

He finally decided to go ahead and call it a night. First he went to the front and looked out the window to see if anyone was lurking around the house. Seeing nobody, he then moved to the back windows and checked outside. Nothing appeared amiss.

He turned off all the lights and made his way to the sofa. He made sure his gun was in easy reach. He shucked his shirt and pants, leaving him in his boxers and stretched out and pulled the blanket over him.

Instantly, a picture of Avery's lips filled his head. He'd lost count of the number of times over the past couple days he'd thought about kissing her, had wanted to kiss her. The next time the desire swept over him he needed to just go for it. Surely if he kissed her once it would get the idea out of his head for good.

He must have fallen asleep, for he awakened with all his senses alert. His hand snaked out of the blanket and grabbed his gun. Something had awakened him—a faint noise, a shift in air pressure…something.

Moonlight drifted into the room, allowing him to see that he was alone. But that didn't mean somebody who didn't belong wasn't in the house.

Without making a sound, he slid off the sofa. His heartbeat slowed as he went into the cool, un-emotional mode that had served him well as a soldier.

He smelled her before he saw her, that evocative scent that dizzied his brain. Avery. He flipped on the living room light, to find her standing at the mouth of the hallway.

"Avery. Jeez, woman, you almost got yourself shot." He lowered his gun. "What in the hell are you doing, skulking around?"

His tone must have been sharper than he intended, for her lower lip trembled. "I'm so sorry. I didn't want to wake you, but apparently the twins don't like pepperoni very much. I've got a little heartburn and so I was just going to get a glass of milk."

"Come on then, let's get those kids some milk." Together they headed for the kitchen, where he turned on the light and sat at the table while she beelined to the refrigerator.

She was clad in a long white cotton nightgown with little blue flowers on it. The low scooped neckline revealed the tops of her breasts and he tried desperately not to focus his attention there.

The clock on the microwave indicated it was a quarter before two. "Do you get heartburn often?" he asked.

"Not too often, but occasionally. I should have known better than to eat all that pepperoni off the pizza." She poured the milk and then joined him at the table. "I really am sorry that I woke you, but I couldn't stand it any longer, and milk seems to be the only thing that works to ease the burning."

"Avery, I don't ever want you to worry about waking me up. You need to go about your normal life and just ignore that I'm in the house."

She took a sip of the milk and then smiled at him. "It's pretty hard to ignore a nearly naked, handsome hunk sleeping on my sofa." Instantly her cheeks grew pink and she quickly stared down into her glass.

"So, you really think I'm a handsome hunk?" he asked teasingly, hoping to stop an awkward moment from happening and ridiculously pleased by her words. He chose to ignore the "nearly naked" part of her comment, although he wished he would have yanked on his jeans before he'd come into the kitchen.

"You know you are," she replied. "Besides, I wouldn't have jumped into bed with you so fast the night we first met if you hadn't swept me off my feet with your physical attractiveness."

"So, are you telling me you're a shallow woman who only sees somebody's outer beauty?" Once again his tone was teasing.

Her eyes sparkled with humor. "Yes, that's exactly what I'm telling you. I am a shallow woman who only surrounds myself with beautiful people."

He laughed. "If you were really that kind of a woman then I wouldn't like you as much as I do."

She held his gaze for a long moment. "It's important that we like each other not only just now, but for a long time to come."

"There's no reason why that isn't going to happen," he replied. "Now, drink your milk so you can go back to bed and get some sleep."

She finished the milk and then put the glass in the dishwasher. He walked with her down the hallway and the scent of her wafted around him. Suddenly his desire burned hot inside him.

Just a kiss. Since the moment he'd seen her again he'd been tormented by memories of what they had shared on the night they had met. He wanted just one kiss to confirm that his memories of kissing her were far better than the actual act.

When they reached her bedroom door, she turned back to look at him. "Again, I'm sorry for waking you," she said.

"No problem." He gave himself no time to over-think things, and no little voice whispered caution in his head. Dallas reached out and took her in his arms and then captured her lips with his.

Sweet heat rushed through him. Her lips were so warm and welcoming, and the kiss was better… far better than his memories. The heat intensified when she opened her mouth to allow him to deepen the kiss. Her tongue swirled with his and created a maelstrom of want in him.

The kiss stirred him to his very depths and reminded him that he was a vital, healthy man who had been without physical touch for a long time. And right now he didn't want to touch anyone but Avery.

Someplace in the back of his mind he knew this was a first step on a road he didn't intend to travel. As much as he desired her, he wouldn't…he couldn't make love with her.

First and foremost, she was almost eight months pregnant and there was no way he'd take a chance at somehow harming the babies. Secondly, becoming her lover was just a bad idea all the way around, considering the relationship they were trying to build as coparents.

With these things working their way through his brain, he finally, reluctantly, broke the kiss and stepped away from her. "Good night, Avery." He didn't wait for a reply, but quickly turned on his heels and headed back up the hallway.

He settled on the sofa and waited for his heart to resume a more normal rhythm. The kiss had been far better than his memory. Her lips had been so much softer and hotter, her body far warmer against his than he'd remembered.

At this point he didn't know what was going to be more difficult, keeping her alive or keeping things in the friends-only zone.

Chapter 8

Avery had just awakened and was still in bed when her cell phone rang the next morning. It was Breanna. "Hey, girlfriend, it's time for a check-in. How are things going?"

Rolling over on her back, Avery checked to make sure her bedroom door was closed and Dallas couldn't overhear her. "Things have gotten a bit strange."

"Strange how?"

Avery explained first about Lulu and then the terrifying car incident. "Breanna, I've never been so frightened in my entire life as when that truck was banging into me."

"Oh my God, Avery. What is Chief Thompson saying about all of it?"

"Not much. He's investigating, so hopefully he'll have some answers about who is responsible soon. In the meantime, Dallas has moved in with me to make sure I stay safe."

"Now, that's really interesting. Still no sparks between the two of you?"

"He's strictly here for my personal safety," Avery replied.

"That doesn't answer my question. Are there sparks?"

"Breanna, it's just not like that between us." Avery tried not to think about the unexpected kiss that had happened the night before.

"Well, that's too bad. It would be a real fairy-tale ending if you and Dallas wound up in love and raising the twins together."

Avery laughed. "You know I don't believe in storybook endings. I've never wanted a man in my life in a meaningful way."

"Avery, you can't let Zeke's death limit your ability to care for people. Your brother wouldn't have wanted that for you. You deserve to have a great man in your life. It would just be nice if that man was Dallas, since you're pregnant with his children."

"And it would be nice if your ex-husband would pay his child support on time, but we both know that's not going to happen," Avery replied with a laugh.

"But I'm glad Dallas is there with you. I hope you're taking the threats against you seriously."

"We're taking it all very seriously," Avery replied. The two friends chatted for another few minutes and then ended the call.

Avery remained in bed, her head whirling with myriad thoughts. The threats made against her swirled around with memories of Zeke. She'd definitely stopped believing in any kind of fairy tales when her brother had died. She had never wanted to love anyone again and then lose him.

Then her brain fired with memories of what had happened at her bedroom doorway the night before. That kiss. It had curled her toes and filled her with a desire for more…for so much more.

Was it so wrong for her to want to make love with the father of her babies? Was it really so wrong for her to want to be in his arms again? He must feel some kind of physical desire for her. After all, he had initiated the kiss.

But she wasn't foolish enough to pretend that the sexual attraction between them meant anything. Desire didn't require love. Love didn't have to exist to feel great passion.

She finally pulled herself out of bed and went into the bathroom for a shower. Were things going to be awkward between them because of the kiss the night before? She certainly hoped not. She finished her shower and dressed for the day, and then went to the kitchen, where she found Dallas seated at the table with a cup of coffee in front of him.

He offered her a smile, and it took only a few minutes for her to realize he was acting like nothing had happened between them, so she did the same. However, that didn't stop her from thinking about it.

They were just finishing breakfast when her phone rang. It was Chad. "Danny and I were wondering if we could drop by and have a cup of coffee and check in on our pregnant girl."

"That would be great," she replied.

"How about in a half an hour or so?"

"Sounds good to me," she stated.

They hung up. "That was Chad. He and Danny are going to stop by for a little visit in about half an hour. Is that okay with you?" she asked Dallas.

"Avery, this is your house and you don't have to ask my permission to have your friends here. Truthfully, I'm looking forward to meeting them, since they helped you out so much when I wasn't in the picture." He finished the last of his coffee and got up from the table.

"They are a couple of great guys. I think you'll like them both. Once they leave I intend to spend the rest of the day on the computer, looking for names for the mummy investigation." She got up as well and together they began to clear the table.

"I plan to do the same," he replied. "The more men we find, the better the odds that we find the killer."

"I know a lot of young women will rest easier knowing this killer is off the streets."

"I'll rest easier when we get whoever is after *you* off the streets," he declared.

A chill shot through her at his words. "Maybe Danny and Chad will know something more about that. They have all kinds of contacts on the streets."

"Then let's hope they have some information about all this," he replied.

With the kitchen clean, they moved into the living room to await the men's arrival. Avery wanted to talk about the kiss. She wanted to know if they were crossing out of the friends-only zone and into something more intimate and a bit more dangerous.

It was probably a bad idea for them to become lovers. That would make it more risky, because if things went south, then bad feelings might occur, and that would be the last thing she wanted for her babies. It was vital that she and Dallas maintain a good, healthy relationship.

She didn't want to have one of *those* relationships with him, where the handoffs of the children were filled with anger or tension. She didn't want to fight about sharing holidays or summer vacations.

Breanna had a toxic relationship with her ex-husband, and Avery had seen the toll it had taken not only on her friend, but also on Breanna's children. There was no way Avery wanted that for herself or the twins.

But knowing that to indulge in an intimate relationship with Dallas wasn't a good idea didn't stop her from wishing things could be different. Just sitting next to him on the sofa and talking about the weather, she found her mind filled with the memory of that hot and wonderful kiss.

Thankfully, Chad and Danny arrived before she could say or do anything stupid about that kiss. She made the introductions and they all shook hands.

"First of all, I'd like to thank you both for everything you've done for Avery," Dallas said.

"We consider her quite special," Chad replied. "Besides, she bullied us into doing most of it."

"Yes, I can be quite the bully," Avery said with a laugh.

"That's not true," Danny protested.

"Now she's on to bullying me," Dallas said, and they all laughed.

For the next few minutes they all visited about the weather and the approach of Halloween, a night that Chad proclaimed to hate. "I try never to be home on Halloween. I don't care about little goblins looking for candy."

"Oh, I love it," Avery said. "It's one of my favorite nights of the year. I think it's such fun to see the kids in their costumes." She looked at Dallas. "Just think, this time next year we'll have two babies to take trick-or-treating."

"And they'll be too young to eat all that candy, so I guess I'll have to help them with that," he said. "It will be a tough job, but somebody's got to do it."

They all laughed again, and warmth filled Avery's heart as she gazed at Dallas. This little look into the future reminded her how much they needed to be sure and get their relationship right. They couldn't screw this up. For the sake of the twins, they absolutely had to get this right.

"We heard about the road rage incident you went through," Chad said, changing the topic to a more serious one. Immediately, a cold wind blew through Avery. It was the chilly wind of residual fear.

"It was more than a case of road rage. It was attempted murder," Dallas said grimly. "She was lucky she kept her head about her when it happened."

"I'm... We're just glad you're okay," Danny interjected.

"She's going to continue to be okay. I've moved in here to make sure of that," Dallas said.

Both men looked surprised. Chad glanced from Dallas to Avery, then gazed back at Dallas. "Whatever it takes to keep her safe, right? She's an important part of our team and aside from that we kind of like her."

She laughed. "Thanks, guys."

"Actually, one of our reasons for stopping by is because I heard a little gossip from one of my snitches on the streets. Last night he told me that Max Malone is behind the attacks on you," Chad said.

"We immediately took that information to Chief Thompson," Danny said.

Dallas looked at her. "Who is this Max Malone?"

"I'm not sure," she replied thoughtfully. "He isn't somebody I have a history with. He's never appeared before me in court."

"He's a two-bit thug who is friends with Joel Asman and Dwayne Conway," Chad replied. "According to my snitch he was bragging about being behind the attack on a poodle. So we can assume he was talking about Lulu."

"I'd like to put him in jail for a hundred years and more for what he did to my dog," Avery replied fervently.

"What about the attack on the road? Have you heard any rumblings about that?" Dallas asked.

"My source couldn't confirm if Max was the man behind the wheel in the truck that tried to run you off the road or not," Chad replied.

"Chief Thompson promised us he'd check Max out," Danny said.

"If he's the one who tormented Lulu, then I hope he gets put in jail sooner rather than later," she replied. She looked at the dog, which was curled up in the bed at the end of the sofa.

For just a moment her brain replayed that moment when she had found Lulu under the bush, shivering and covered with what she'd thought was blood. Another icy wind blew through her. She'd thought for sure Lulu was on the verge of death.

Unfortunately, the perp wouldn't go to jail for what

he had done to Lulu. He'd only be subject to a fine. As an animal lover, Avery found this a glitch in the criminal system that infuriated her. Still, Max might not go to jail for abusing Lulu, but he could certainly serve plenty of time behind bars for threatening a prosecutor, and that note tied around Lulu's neck had definitely been a threat.

Danny and Chad stayed and visited for a few more minutes and then the two men left.

"You know Danny is in love with you," Dallas said, after he'd closed and locked the door behind them.

"I don't know that at all," she immediately protested. "I'll admit I think he might have a little bit of a crush on me," she added, after a moment of thought.

"It's bigger than a crush. Trust me, that man is absolutely crazy in love with you."

"I think you're crazy to even think that," she said with a laugh. She sobered. "I have never given him any indication that I want anything more from him than a friendly coworker relationship." She picked up the coffee cups Danny and Chad had used and carried them into the kitchen.

Dallas followed behind her. "In any case, they both seem like good men."

"They are and I'm so glad you like them," she replied.

"I'm going to grab my computer. Do you mind if I set up here on the table? I can move when it's time for meals."

"Not a problem," she replied. "And I'm going to get busy on my computer, too."

"If we don't hear from him, I'm going to call Chief Thompson later today and see what he can tell me about this Max character, and if they've figured out anything after examining your car."

She frowned. "I just can't believe somebody who has never appeared before me in court is coming after me so hard."

"Apparently putting away Conway stirred up all the cockroaches," he replied. "I'll be right back." He left the room to retrieve his laptop.

The afternoon passed with both of them on their computers. Even though he was in the kitchen and she was in the living room, Avery was acutely conscious of Dallas's presence.

Despite sitting in another room, she could swear she smelled his scent, one of minty soap and fresh cologne that had somehow become identified to her as safety.

They took a break to eat a light lunch, and then at five o'clock knocked off for dinner. She'd made a chicken and rice casserole with a salad and green beans.

After dinner they settled on the sofa together to relax and watch a little television. It had been a good day, and although her lower back hurt, she didn't feel exhausted like she usually did by this time of night.

She found herself wondering why Dallas had indicated to her he wasn't interested in a long-term relationship. He was hot and had a great personality. He seemed to be financially stable, so why wouldn't he want to be married and have a family?

She now found herself curious about why he wouldn't want a partner at his side through life. She knew her own motivation for making such a decision, but what was his?

"Dallas, can I ask you something personal?"

He turned to look at her. "Of course."

"Why aren't you looking to fall in love and get married?" she asked. "I know you're going to be a great father, but I think you'd make some woman a great husband, too. Why have you chosen not to get married?"

Immediately, tension wafted from him. His shoulders went rigidly straight and his gaze shot to the wall behind her head. For just a moment he didn't speak, but his breathing sounded quick and erratic to her.

He frowned and raked a hand through his hair. "I had a wife…my soul mate and my one true love, and I buried her."

Avery gasped. "Oh, Dallas, I'm so very sorry. I had no idea."

He finally turned to look at her. His eyes were a dark, midnight blue as he shrugged. "It happened… I'm over it, but I don't want to ever go through something like that again. I'm fine living the rest of my life alone."

"How did she die? Was she ill?" She hadn't even known he'd been married. She wasn't sure why, but she wanted to know about the woman who had been his soul mate and his one true love.

Once again his gaze shot across the room. "Ivy was healthy as a horse. She was a soldier, and on her last tour of duty in Afghanistan the Jeep she was traveling in ran over an IED. Two other soldiers were hurt, but the blast killed her."

As he spoke his voice had deepened…thickened with obvious emotion.

"Oh, Dallas," Avery said softly.

She knew what it felt like to tragically lose a loved one. She knew the hollow emptiness, the gnawing pain that seemed relentless. Granted, Zeke had been her brother and not her husband, but loss was loss.

"We'd planned to buy a house and really start our life together when she got home. We talked about the family we wanted. We dreamed about our life together." His voice broke.

"I'm so very sorry for your loss, Dallas," she murmured.

Once again he looked away from her. "It was so damned sudden. One moment I was a husband and knew exactly what my future held, and the next moment I just wasn't, and all my hopes and plans had been destroyed."

He drew in a deep breath and released it slowly. "I decided then that I would never marry again, that I didn't want to be somebody else's husband, and I don't think I'll ever change my mind about that. I found my one, true soul mate and she died."

Avery placed a hand on his thigh, wanting to comfort him but not even sure if he wanted her comfort. He remained perfectly still for a long moment and then he covered her hand with his and turned to look at her.

His eyes were still dark, but there was something else besides pain there…something that made her breath catch in the back of her throat.

"These babies…they were like a gift from God for me," he said. His voice was filled with a different emotion than it had been moments before. "And despite my love for Ivy and the fact that I never want to marry again, Avery, I have an enormous desire for you." He released her hand.

She stared at him as her heart began to beat a rhythm of uncertain anticipation. "Dallas, I have the same wild desire for you." The words whispered out of her. "I think I've wanted you since the moment I saw you again."

"So, what are we going to do about this?" His eyes bored into hers.

"I don't know…" She barely got the words out of her mouth when his lips crashed down on hers. The kiss fired a welcomed heat through her. She opened her mouth to allow him entry. The tip of his tongue first touched her lower lip and then entered to dance with hers.

Oh, she wanted this man. She wanted him in her bed, his naked body moving against hers. Her body... Good grief, how could he want her when she was so huge?

She pulled her lips away from his. "Dallas, I want you. I want you to make love to me, but I don't look the same as I did the last time we were together." She looked down at her belly. "I'm fat, and I'll understand if that's a big turnoff for you."

His gaze burned into her. "Oh, Avery, you aren't fat, you're pregnant with my children. I find you and your body incredibly beautiful."

Her heart fluttered at his words...wonderful words that only made her desire for him grow more intense. Surely they could both be adults about this. Surely they could explore the crazy desire between them and still make healthy and good decisions about their children and their relationship.

She got up from the sofa and held out her hand to him. "Please, Dallas, please come and make love to me. I want you so badly."

He remained seated for a long moment, his gaze locked with hers. Finally, he rose and took her hand. Without another word spoken they walked down the hallway to her bedroom.

Lulu padded after them, but once Avery and Dallas crossed the threshold she closed the door, leaving the poodle in the hallway.

Once again they kissed, a searing kiss that, for her, sealed the very rightness of what they were about to share. This couldn't be wrong... It just couldn't be.

When the kiss ended she stepped back from him. Her fingers trembled as she began to unbutton the pale pink blouse she wore. She'd managed to unfasten the second button when he moved closer and gently pushed her hands away.

His gaze was like a hot caress as he finished unbuttoning her blouse and then gently pushed it off her shoulders. It fell to the floor, a pool of discarded pink cotton. He then pulled his polo shirt over his head and tossed it to a corner.

Oh my, she had forgotten the muscled perfection of his chest. But that chest was right in front of her and she couldn't help the way her hands ached to roam freely over the warm, firm skin.

Instead, she moved to one side of the bed. She quickly took off her maternity jeans and then slid beneath the bedsheet wearing only a pair of silk panties and bra. Twilight drifted through the nearby window, painting Dallas in shades of rich gold and faint purple light.

She watched hungrily as he unfastened his jeans and stepped out of them. Then, clad only in a pair of black boxers, he got into the bed with her.

Immediately, he pulled her into his arms for another kiss. His near-naked body was so wonderfully warm against hers and the fever of want grew higher and higher inside her. She'd been thinking so much about the night they had shared her desire to repeat the experience was overwhelming.

The kiss lingered and then he moved his lips down the side of her throat. A moan issued from her at the slow slide of his mouth. His hands cupped her bra-covered breasts. She could feel the heat of his palms through the material and her nipples hardened in response.

She caressed his broad back in turn, enjoying the play of his firm muscles beneath the skin. His scent enticed her. Everything about him at this moment brought all her senses enormous pleasure.

He reached behind her and unfastened her bra. She rose up slightly to aid him as he plucked it off her and tossed it to the same corner where he'd thrown his polo shirt. Then his hands were back on her bare breasts. His thumbs teased and tormented her nipples and she gasped at the sweet sensations that raced through her.

"Avery," he murmured against her skin. "You are so beautiful." He kissed her down her pregnant stomach and stopped at the edge of her panties. He then continued back up her stomach and to her breasts once again.

She tangled her hands in his hair as intense pleasure continued to course through her. The last time she had made love with a man, it had been with Dallas, and she felt as if she'd been just waiting, her body yearning for him and only him ever since.

It didn't matter what happened tomorrow. Somehow, some way they'd figure it out. Tonight, right at this place in time, she didn't want to think about what was rational or right. She didn't want to worry about recriminations or regrets. She just wanted to be in this moment with him and their desire for each other.

Once again he kissed slowly down her stomach. Inch by inch he worked his way to the edge of her panties, only this time when he reached them, he tugged at them to take them off her. She raised her hips to help him, wanting...needing him to touch her as intimately as a man could touch a woman.

Her heart felt as if it was going to explode out of her chest. In this moment she couldn't imagine ever making love to another man. Dallas was the only one she would ever want.

She plucked at his boxers, wanting him as naked as she was. He got the message, for he quickly got out of them. She reached down and took him into her hand. He was hard, but his skin was velvety soft.

He gasped as she moved her hand up and down his length. He moaned deep and low in the back of his throat, and she loved that sound, loved knowing she was giving him pleasure.

He allowed her to stroke him only a brief time and

then he pushed her hand away and instead began to caress her at her very core.

She moved her hips up and down to meet each of his touches, any rational thought that might have been left leaving her mind as she gave herself to the mind-blowing sensations that rushed through her.

Wave after wave of sweet pleasure swept over her, through her, each time bringing her closer and closer to a pinnacle she desperately wanted to reach. And then she was there, shuddering with unbelievable sensations as she cried out his name.

"I need you now, Dallas. I need you to take me now."

He hovered over her, but hesitated. His eyes gleamed in the near darkness of the room. "I'm good, Avery. I—I don't need this. I don't want to hurt you."

"You won't hurt me," she said. "I promise you won't hurt anyone. I want you, Dallas. I want you inside me."

He closed his eyes and for a moment she thought he was going to roll off her. But when he looked at her again it was as he slowly entered her. He kept himself off her stomach but angled to allow their intimacy.

She hissed with pleasure as he began to stroke in and out of her. Her hands roved over his shoulders and then locked on his bulging biceps, loving the feel of his warm skin beneath her palms.

She thrust her hips to meet his strokes and soon

they were moving in a fever pitch. Their breaths became pants and she felt herself climbing up to that precipice once again.

They reached it together. As he spilled into her, she cried out with her own release. He held himself poised above her for a long moment and in the dim light she could see the rapt expression on his face.

He lowered his head for one last, lingering kiss and then rolled off to her side. "Wow," he said softly.

"Double wow," she replied. Sex with him seven and a half months ago had been amazing, but this love-making had been even better. She giggled suddenly. "We sound like a couple of teenagers who have never had sex before."

He raised up on one elbow and stroked his hand over her belly. "I think this proves we've had sex before." He placed his lips close to her stomach. "Everyone okay in there?"

Avery giggled once again. "Trust me, everyone is just fine." Once again he stroked his hand back and forth on her stomach as if caressing the babies inside.

"If you keep that up, you'll put me right to sleep," she said.

He caressed her stomach one last time, and in the semidarkness she saw the smile on his face fade. She sensed that he was about to say something that would ruin the moment. And the last thing she wanted to talk about at this time was that he thought what had just happened was a mistake.

Before that could happen, she rolled away from him and got off the bed. "I'll be back," she murmured, and then went into her bathroom.

She cleaned up and pulled on her long nightgown and a lightweight robe. Even after that her heart was still beating an unnatural rhythm.

You can't be in love with him, she told her reflection in the mirror. Loving Dallas would definitely be a complication in their coparenting relationship. She refused to be in love with him, but at the moment she felt closer to him than any other man who had ever been in her life.

It wasn't that she was falling in love with Dallas; it was just that there was no question she loved making love with him. Her body definitely liked his and she told herself there was nothing wrong with that. What they had just shared changed nothing between them.

She left her bathroom to find Dallas standing at the foot of the bed. He'd pulled on his jeans, but must have been interrupted by a phone call, for he had his cell pressed to his ear.

"No…no, I can't," he said to whoever was on the other end. "No, I've got Avery to think about."

"What's going on?" Avery asked. She wouldn't have asked if she hadn't heard her name.

"Hang on, Donovan," he said into the phone, then turned to her. "There's a lost little boy out on the Miller ranch, but they can find him without me."

"No," she replied. "You go on, I'll be just fine here."

She could see how torn he was from the deep frown that etched across his forehead. "Please, Dallas," she pressed. "Search and rescue, that's what you do. Now go and help bring that little boy home."

He hesitated only a moment and then spoke into the phone once again. "Okay, Donovan, I'll be out there as soon as I can get geared up. Yeah…Okay, then I'll meet you there."

He clicked off and tossed the phone on the bed, and then pulled his shirt over his head. "Are you sure you'll be okay here?"

"I'll be fine," she assured him. "I've got the alarm system and I have no plans to open the door to anyone."

He grabbed his phone and tucked it into his back pocket. Together they left the bedroom and went back into the living room, where he collected his keys and his gun off one of the end tables.

He turned back to her at the front door. "Make sure you reset the alarm, and call 911 if anything happens."

"Nothing is going to happen," she insisted. "I feel completely safe in the house. It's only when I'm out of it that I feel at risk. Now go."

Once he was gone she reset the alarm system and then walked over to the sofa and sank down into the cushions. Lulu immediately danced at her feet and whined, as if upset she'd been ignored for so long.

Avery picked her up and placed her on the sofa

at her side. Lulu put her head on Avery's thigh and gazed up at her as if seeking answers to questions that Avery didn't have. Questions like what her real feelings were where Dallas was concerned.

Since her brother's death, she had been so certain she didn't want a real relationship with a man in her life. But Breanna's words suddenly played in her mind, reminding her that Zeke wouldn't have wanted her to spend her life alone. He would have wished love for her.

Now, as she looked into her future, she wasn't so sure that being without a man, a soul mate, was what she wanted, and her change of heart was all about Dallas.

But it had been only a little bit earlier in the evening that he had told her about his wife and his decision never to marry again. He'd had his soul mate and so surely he couldn't be Avery's.

At the moment she couldn't trust any of her feelings. Her life was in turmoil. She had threats hanging over her head, and the desire to help catch a serial killer. Her hormones were probably all crazy. The last thing she needed to do right now was trust her own judgment about anything.

She leaned her head back and closed her eyes as her brain replayed in slow motion what she and Dallas had just shared. He had satiated her, but with his scent lingering on her skin and her lips imprinted with his, she wanted him all over again.

And that scared her. Because despite everything she had just told herself, she now realized her biggest challenge was going to be stopping herself from falling in love with her babies' father.

Chapter 9

Donovan and Forrest were waiting for Dallas when he arrived on horseback at the Miller ranch. Dallas had gone to his place and saddled up his horse, Scout. He'd grabbed the gear used for search and rescue and then ridden to the Miller place, which wasn't far from the Colton ranch. Forrest was also on horseback and Donovan was in a truck. There were other neighbors who had come to help, as well.

David and Holly Miller were frantic. With a total of five children, they hadn't noticed when their seven-year-old had slipped out of the house. Michael, the missing little boy, had told his brother that he was going out to find some blackberries.

Darkness had fallen and Michael hadn't returned.

The family had already checked the entire house and the barn, but there was no sign of him.

"As far as I know there aren't any blackberry bushes on the property," David said worriedly.

"Then what would make him go look for them?" Donovan asked.

"It has to be because of the book I read to him last night before bedtime," Holly said tearfully. "It was about a magic land behind a blackberry bush." She began to cry again and her husband threw an arm around her shoulders. "I should have never read him that book. This is all my fault."

David pulled his slender wife against his side. "Honey, you couldn't have known what Michael would do."

"Please, just find him," she cried. "He's out there all alone in the night, and he's afraid of the dark."

Dallas felt gutted as he imagined the horror he would feel if one of his twins went missing. He couldn't imagine what Holly and David were going through. He hoped like hell nothing tragic had happened to the boy.

It took only a few minutes for the men to organize a plan and then they left the house. Dallas got back on Scout, settled into his saddle and pulled out his high-powered flashlight. At least they were lucky in that the moon was full and bright, and spilled down some illumination over the landscape.

"Michael," Dallas called, as Scout walked slowly away from the house toward the pasture in the distance.

On either side of him Dallas could see the flashlights and hear the cries of the other searchers as they called the little boy's name. They all moved slowly, wanting to make sure that each and every part of the property was checked out.

Thankfully, there was no reason to believe that the child had been abducted. Holly and David hadn't seen anyone lurking around their house and Michael had indicated to his brother that he was leaving the house.

So where did a little boy go to look for blackberry bushes? How far could he have walked? Far enough to lose his bearings and get lost? Dallas guessed that's probably what had happened. Hopefully, Michael would hear them calling for him and answer.

Minutes ticked by…long minutes that eventually turned into half an hour and then an hour. They passed several outbuildings, and checked them thoroughly, but no little boy was found inside.

There was nothing worse than a missing child. The event could galvanize a community, and as time went on more and more people joined the search. The flashlights of the searchers looked like dozens of fireflies lighting the night.

Dallas had just ridden near a ravine that led to a dry streambed when he thought he heard a faint cry. He drew Scout to a halt and listened. Had it been an animal he'd heard? He couldn't be sure.

He urged Scout closer to the edge. "Michael," he shouted once again.

"It's me. I'm down here," a faint little voice replied. "Somebody help me!"

Dallas released a deep sigh of relief. He called Donovan on his cell phone. "I found him. He's down in a ravine."

"Is he okay?"

"He's talking so I think he's fine," Dallas replied.

"I'll send some men your way and I'll head back to the house to let his parents know," Donovan replied. He had told David and Holly to remain at the house while the more professional search and rescue team were working. Besides if Michael wound up back at the house on his own, he might want his mommy and daddy there.

"Help me," Michael yelled again. "Is somebody up there?"

"I'm here, buddy," Dallas replied. He pocketed his phone, dismounted and led Scout closer. "Michael, my name is Dallas and I'm here to help you. Can you come up?"

"I can't. I hurt my ankle. I—I can't stand up. It hurts." The sound of the boy's weeping rose up from the ravine.

"It's okay, Michael. Don't cry. I'll come down and get you," Dallas replied. "We'll get you back to your mom and dad in no time. They've been very worried about you."

Dallas turned to Scout and from the saddlebag pulled the first aid kit he carried when doing search and rescues. He opened it and pulled out a roll of elastic wrap. He had no idea how badly Michael had hurt his ankle, but Dallas intended to wrap it before he brought the boy up.

Although the ravine sides were fairly steep, there was no need for any special equipment to get down to the bottom. Gripping his flashlight firmly, Dallas began his descent. His feet nearly slid out from beneath him as loose stones and dirt clods rolled downward.

When he reached the bottom, he shone his flashlight toward a small figure seated on the ground— a blond little boy with big blue eyes that wept great big tears.

"Hi, Michael. How did you get down here?" Dallas sat on the ground next to the child.

"I just wanted to see if there was any blackberry bushes down here, but when I started to walk down, I hurt my ankle and tumbled to the bottom and then I couldn't get back up. Are you mad at me?"

"Nah, I'm not mad at you," Dallas replied. "Did you hurt yourself anyplace else besides your ankle?"

"I skinned up my elbow a little bit."

"Let me see." Dallas trained his flashlight on the boy's elbow, which was indeed skinned up, but it was nothing serious.

"I'll bet my mom and dad are mad at me," Michael said, his voice trembling with the promise of tears once again.

"I think they just want you home with them. They love you very much. Now, let me take a look at that ankle."

It was swollen, and although Dallas didn't believe anything was broken, it was definitely sprained. "When I try to stand on it, it hurts awful bad." Michael began to cry again. "I thought nobody was ever going to find me down here and my bones would just turn to dust and I'd blow away."

"Well, that's not going to happen now," Dallas said. He wrapped the ankle and then got up on his haunches. "Can you get on me, piggyback?"

The boy maneuvered himself until he was clinging to Dallas's back.

"Hang on tight. We're going up."

Several other flashlights shone from above, letting Dallas know some of the other searchers had arrived. "Dallas, do you need a rope or any help?" Forrest called.

"No, I think I'm okay." It didn't take too much effort for him to get up to the top, where his horse was waiting. He placed Michael on the saddle and then mounted up behind him. "Let's get you home."

He wrapped his arms around the little boy as they headed back to the house. There would come a time when he'd have his son or his daughter on a horse in

front of him just like this. The thought shot yet another thrill of fatherhood through him.

When they reached the house, Dallas dismounted,
plucked Michael off the horse and carried him up the
front steps.

"You can put him right in here," Holly said, and
gestured them into the living room and to the sofa.
Dallas followed her, along with several of the other
men.

The minute Dallas attempted to place the boy
down, Michael's arms tightened around his neck.
"Thank you, Mr. Dallas, for not letting me be lost
forever. Thank you for not letting my bones blow to
the wind." He kissed Dallas on the cheek and then
released his hold on him.

Dallas straightened, his heart touched by the sweet
kiss he'd just received. Holly immediately moved to
her son's side and pulled him into her arms.

"You might want to get a doctor to check out his
ankle," Dallas said. "I think it's just sprained, but an
x-ray wouldn't be a bad idea."

"We'll take care of that," David said. He shook
everyone's hand and thanked them all profusely.

Minutes later Dallas was riding back to his place to
stable his horse and then get back to Avery's. Thank
God this search and rescue had a happy ending. Thank
God the boy's injuries hadn't been more severe.

Dallas had a feeling little Michael had two things
in his near future: a better ankle wrap and a lecture

from his parents about leaving the house without permission.

Now that the rescue had been resolved, Dallas's head filled with thoughts of Avery and what had happened between them before he'd left the house.

Making love with her again had been as hot and as magical as the first time they'd been together. In fact, this time had been much better, because he did care about Avery, where the first time she'd been nothing but a tempting stranger.

He shoved those thoughts away. With the adrenaline from the search ebbing, he was just too tired to try to sort out his feelings about Avery.

It was almost two when he softly knocked on her front door, cursing the fact that he didn't have a key and couldn't get inside without disturbing her.

It took three knocks before she finally came to the door to let him in. Her hair was tousled and her eyes were at half-mast with sleep, but she offered him a beautiful smile and asked him about the missing child.

"He was found and is back home safely with his parents," he told her. "Now, go back to bed."

She didn't argue with him. As she headed down the hallway to her bedroom, with Lulu at her heels, he fought the desire to go with her and curl up in her bed with her in his arms.

Instead he headed for the sofa. As he settled in for sleep, he realized she must have been sleeping there while waiting for him. Her scent lingered on the pillow and in the blanket.

He breathed in her sweet fragrance and within minutes he was asleep.

He woke just after dawn, despite the fact that he hadn't gotten back to Avery's house until after two in the morning.

Although he was wide-awake, he remained on the sofa. It would be hours before Avery got up. Before she did, he needed to figure out what he would say or even if he was going to speak to her about what had happened between them the night before.

He told himself that he'd fallen into bed with her because the conversation about Ivy had stirred up old memories and had created a deep pool of grief inside him, and all he'd wanted was to be with Avery to take away his pain over his dead wife. All he'd needed was warmth and passion to take away some of the ache. It could have been any woman, he told himself firmly.

But he suspected he was lying to himself. There was only one reason he'd made love with Avery, and that was because he'd wanted to. It was as simple and as complicated as that. Last night he'd acted on a desire for her that had been burning inside him since the moment he'd seen her again. His passion had been for Avery, and for Avery alone.

Now that he'd acted on that desire, he had hoped

it would go away. But it hadn't. Instead it had merely stirred more passion for her inside him.

And it had to stop. He had to stop. By making love with Avery he was jeopardizing his future with her and his children. He couldn't take the risk of things going south with her. He hoped they could get back on track with a friendship-only relationship despite what had happened between them the night before.

When she got up they had to have a conversation about it. He had to tell her that it had all been a big mistake.

He finally roused himself from the sofa and padded to the guest bathroom. He took a quick shower and then went to the kitchen to make himself coffee.

He sat at the table, and as he drank the fresh brew his mind filled with other troubling thoughts. First and foremost, he wanted whoever was after Avery behind bars. But that wasn't the only thing that concerned him.

Last night, after they'd found Michael and before he had left the Miller ranch, he had spoken with both his brothers. Donovan had told him how frustrated everyone was about the lack of leads in the mummy case.

There had been seven women killed forty years ago. The murderer had been caught and had died behind bars. But the newest murders tied back to that old crime. Somehow law enforcement had missed something.

Dallas knew Chief Thompson and his men were doing everything in their power to investigate, but already the cases had stalled out and no new information was coming in.

What he hated more than anything was the fear that filled the young women in Whisperwood. Forrest had told him that after dark the streets of the town were nearly deserted, as women locked themselves in their homes for safety.

What had they missed before? What were they missing now? Elliot Corgan had gone to prison for the murders of the women. Was it possible the wrong man had been convicted? Unfortunately, they couldn't go back and re-interview Elliot. There was no way to question a dead man.

Had he really hanged himself? Had guilt caused him to take his own life? Or had he been "helped" to his death in order to protect somebody else?

Dallas was on his third cup of coffee when Avery made her appearance. She looked lovely in a green blouse that complemented her eyes and a pair of jeans that hugged her slender legs. She smelled of minty soap and the evocative fragrance that always stirred him.

"Good morning," she greeted him as she went to the cupboard to grab a cup for tea.

"Good morning to you," he replied. "And how are Jack and Jill this morning?"

She laughed. "They're good."

He watched as she made her tea and then sat in the chair opposite his. "You slept well?"

"After you got back home, I slept like a baby," she replied. "What about you?"

"I slept okay," he said.

"So, tell me what happened last night. You said you found the little boy. Where was he?"

He told her about finding Michael at the bottom of the ravine and that the little boy had been looking for a blackberry bush. "All I could think about was if someday my son got lost, I'd hope a lot of people would look for him until he was found."

"Let's hope neither of our children ever get lost," she replied. "And let's agree that we will never read our kids a book about a magical land behind a blackberry bush."

"I totally agree," he replied.

He cupped his hands around his cup, hating the conversation he needed to have with her. "Avery, we need to talk about last night."

"What about it?" Her eyes suddenly held a soft vulnerability. "Dallas, before you say anything, I want you to know that for me it was more than wonderful."

He frowned and looked down into his coffee cup. Damn, but he wished she hadn't said that. That was only going to make this conversation more difficult.

"Was it not so wonderful for you?" she asked softly.

He jerked his gaze back to her. "No... I mean, yes. It was wonderful, but you know we can't do that again."

"I don't expect anything from you. We could make love a dozen times and I still wouldn't want anything from you except that you be a terrific father to our babies."

Oh, he wished she'd stop looking at him with such sweet yearning. He wished she hadn't said they could make love a bunch more times and their relationship would remain static. It wouldn't. Relationships didn't stay static and he was still adamant that he didn't want to marry again.

There was no future for them as romantic partners and he was afraid that eventually, no matter what she said, he would hurt her, and then things would get awkward and difficult.

"Avery, I just think it's better if we don't go there again," he finally said. "We both know that's not the kind of relationship we need to have."

She was silent for several long moments. "Okay, whatever you want," she finally replied, although he thought he heard both regret and disappointment in her voice. This time she broke their gaze and looked down into her teacup.

God, already he felt like a total heel. He wanted to take back his words, but he couldn't. They had needed to be said.

"How about some breakfast?" She looked back at him. "I feel like an omelet."

"That sounds great to me." He breathed an inward sigh of relief that the conversation about them making love was over.

As they ate, they talked about their favorite breakfast foods. "I'll confess, I'm a big fan of biscuits and gravy," he said. "Although a cheese omelet with sides of bacon and toast run a close second." He gestured to the food before him.

"Pancakes," she replied. "Pancakes dripping with butter and syrup."

"Waffles with strawberries and powdered sugar."

She grinned at him. "Eggs Benedict."

"Eggs over easy."

She laughed. "We sound like we're playing some game of food wars."

He grinned at her. "Then I declare myself the winner of the game."

"Whoa, what made you the winner?" Her eyes sparkled merrily.

"Trust me, when it comes to food games, I'll always be the winner."

"Okay, I'll give you this win," she replied. "But that doesn't mean you get to win all the battles. We'll see who is best at changing a diaper."

He was grateful that she seemed fine after the talk they'd had, and had even teased him. The good vibes between them continued as they finished up the meal and then moved to their computers. One of the things Dallas found so surprising was how very comfortable he felt around Avery.

Despite what had happened between them the night before and the rather tough conversation he'd had with her this morning, he felt as if they were building a strong friendship.

He found her ability to get silly absolutely charming. He also liked having serious conversations with her about parenting and politics, about world views and personal goals.

He'd have to get over the fact that there were times when she gazed at him and his heart stepped up its rhythm, or that the scent of her stirred him on a level that had nothing to do with friendship.

It concerned him that for the past couple days he'd been unable to remember Ivy's smile. Every time he tried to pull up her smiling countenance, he saw only Avery's.

He didn't want to ever forget his wife, the woman he had pledged his life to. The last thing he wanted to do was diminish how much he'd loved Ivy. He needed her in his heart.

He cleared his head of all thoughts as he got to work. Donovan had also told him the night before that Chief Thompson and his men were stretched to their limits. They were not only working the murder investigations, but also on the growing drug issue in Whisperwood.

Dallas and Avery worked until noon and then

stopped for a lunch of sandwiches and chips. When they were finished she got up from the table and placed her hands on her lower back and winced.

"Back bothering you?" he asked.

"Yes, Popeye and Olive seem to be riding me pretty hard at the moment."

He smiled at her use of old cartoon characters' names. "Do you want to stretch out on the sofa and I'll give you a quick massage?"

Her eyes lit up. "Oh, Dallas, that would be wonderful. Would you mind?"

"I wouldn't have offered if I minded," he replied.

However, the minute she got comfortable on her side on the sofa and he began to massage her lower back, he wanted to take back his offer.

She moaned with pleasure as he worked his hands and kneaded her warm, bare skin. Her face was turned away from him and her eyes were closed.

It would be so easy for him to lean forward and kiss her cheek. It would be so incredibly easy to slide his hands up and unfasten her bra and start something he had no business starting.

He focused on the massage for another couple minutes and then backed away from her. "Better?" he asked, as he helped her into a sitting position.

"Much better. Thank you."

"I'm going to get back to the computer," he said. He went into the kitchen, grateful for the small distance from her. He settled back at the table to work and assumed Avery was doing the same in the living room.

That was the routine they fell into over the next week. They shared breakfast and then surfed the web until lunchtime. After lunch he worked some more on hunting down soldiers and she often took a nap.

Chad and Danny popped in for another visit, but had nothing to add about the threats against Avery. Chad talked about some of the cases they were prosecuting and asked Avery for her advice.

As Dallas listened to Avery talking with her co-workers, he was once again struck by her intelligence and her passion for her work. He knew that eventually, after the twins were born, she intended to go back to work, and he was on board with that. There was no doubt in his mind that she could be a great mother and a great prosecutor at the same time.

They now sat side by side on the sofa as another day wound down. Lulu was in Dallas's lap, curled up and happy as he stroked his hand down her back.

Dallas didn't know when he'd felt such contentment. There was such a sense of peace inside him, a peace that he knew had to do with Avery.

This place had begun to feel more like home than his own cabin. Here was warmth and laughter and the anticipation of the future with his babies.

His cabin had come to represent loneliness and isolation. He dreaded the time when he'd go back there. Hopefully, when the twins were born and he could take them to the cabin, he'd feel differently about the place he called home.

Twice in the past week he and Avery had left the house, once to get some groceries and then to retrieve her car from the authorities. Both times he sensed no danger surrounding her. Thankfully, the outings had been uneventful.

The most difficult thing he'd had to battle over the past week had been his growing feelings for the mother of his children.

It wasn't enough that he desired Avery with an energy that burned within him night and day. He was shocked by the level of affection he felt toward her. He loved being around her. She charmed him with her laughter and he wanted to know what she was thinking when she grew pensive.

He liked their conversations and enjoyed the quiet time they shared. Yes, the truth was she and this place had begun to feel like home. And it wasn't his home. He had to keep reminding himself that this was just a temporary resting place in his crazy life.

"I think I'm ready to call it a night," Avery said, when the show they had been watching ended. She got up from the sofa. "I wonder if it's raining?" It had been a cloudy day with overnight rain in the forecast.

He watched as she moved to the window and peered outside. Instantly, her entire body stiffened. "Dallas," she whispered. "There's somebody outside.

I—I think it's Joel Asman." She turned around to face Dallas, her face a sickly shade of white. "Why is he here? What's he doing out there?"

Dallas grabbed his gun. "Lock the door behind me," he said urgently, and then flew out the front door.

He immediately saw Joel standing on the sidewalk. Joel instantly took off running and Dallas gave chase. He had hoped the heat was off Avery, but Joel's presence now said otherwise.

What in the hell was the man up to? Joel stayed on the sidewalk for only a few seconds and then veered off across people's grassy yards. Dallas followed him, damning the cloud cover that made vision difficult.

Remembering this was the man who had knocked into Avery at the diner and whose name had come up as a thug friend of Dwayne Conway, Dallas desperately wanted to catch him.

A dog barked in the distance as the two of them ran through a backyard. He didn't want to fire his gun. Joel hadn't broken any laws by standing on the sidewalk outside Avery's house, but if he was perfectly honest with himself, Dallas would admit he wouldn't mind beating the tar out of him for scaring Avery.

Joel jumped over a fence, and Dallas was about to leap over it in pursuit of the creep when a sudden, horrifying thought struck him. What had Joel been doing in front of Avery's house? Absolutely nothing. He'd just been standing there, apparently waiting to be seen.

So Dallas would chase after him? So somebody else hiding in the backyard could break into the house? His heart stuttered to a stop at the thought.

Avery was alone in the place. Was some murderous thug right now breaking in? Oh God. He turned on his heels and headed back toward the house, his heart now thundering with panic. Had he just fallen into a trap? Had he made it easy for somebody to get to Avery?

God, he needed to get home. He needed to get to Avery. His panting breaths nearly choked him as he pushed himself, running as fast as he'd ever run in his life.

Avery! Her name thundered in his head over and over again. He had to get home to her. She had to be okay. He'd never forgive himself if anything happened to her.

He ran even harder as the house came into view. When he reached it he banged on the front door. When she opened it, he gasped her name and pulled her into a tight embrace.

"Thank God," he said into her hair. "Thank God you're okay." It was at that moment he realized he was starting to fall in love with the mother of his children.

Chapter 10

Avery and Dallas had just finished breakfast the next morning when a knock sounded on her door. It was Chief Thompson. Dallas let him in and offered him a cup of coffee. He had called the chief the night before about Asman's appearance in front of the house.

"I'd love a cup of coffee," Archer replied, and sank down in the chair facing the sofa.

Avery got him a cup and then she and Dallas sat on the sofa and waited for the lawman to speak.

"I'm sorry, I've been very remiss in checking in with you two," Archer said, and then paused to take a sip of his coffee.

"No need to apologize," Avery assured him. "We know how much you have on your plate right now."

"I had a little chat this morning with Joel Asman," Archer said. "He's a nasty punk."

"What did he have to say about showing up here last night?" Dallas asked.

"That it's a free country and he could stand on any sidewalk in town and it wasn't breaking any law," Archer replied. "I think he just wanted to rattle your cage," he said to Avery.

"If that was his goal, then he succeeded," Avery replied drily. She looked at Dallas, remembering how frantic he had been when he'd returned to the house after chasing Joel down the street.

"Unfortunately, he's right. I can't arrest him for being on the sidewalk," Chief Thompson said. "On another note, we're still on the outlook for the black pickup truck that rammed into you."

He'd already told them that from the damage on Avery's car they had been able to identify the offending truck as black. Unfortunately, the men in the area who had black pickups had no reason to come after Avery, and Max Malone, the initial suspect, had no vehicle at all licensed in his name.

"Somebody has stashed that truck in a barn or shed someplace," Dallas said in frustration. "It's got to have some front-end damage."

"And Joel Asman alibied Max for the time of the truck attack," Chief Thompson added.

"So, we really can't be sure those two were behind the previous attacks," Dallas said.

"According to Chad's street sources they were the two who were trash-talking after the Conway trial," Archer replied. "So it wouldn't be a surprise if they were behind the attacks, but unfortunately, I have no proof." He took another sip of his coffee.

"For the day the note was tied around your dog's neck, Joel Asman and Max Malone alibied each other. It was the same when the truck rammed into you. So far I've been unable to break their alibis. And that's where things are right now." Chief Thompson's frustration was rife in his voice.

"Thank you for everything you're doing," Avery said.

Archer stood and drained the last of his coffee. "I'm damned sorry I don't have anything for you right now."

Dallas and Avery stood, as well. "Still, we appreciate you coming by," Avery said, as she took the coffee cup from him.

"I'll walk you out," Dallas said.

As the two men headed for the front door, Avery carried the cup back to the kitchen. She was disappointed that Archer hadn't had any answers for them.

Dallas had been in her home for almost two weeks now, and for the past couple days Avery had been arguing with herself about what needed to occur.

She wasn't sure when it had happened, but at

some point during the past little while she had fallen deeply, crazily in love with Dallas.

And with each day that passed her love for him only grew. He was the dream she'd never known she had... Their life together was the fantasy that she now desperately wished was a reality.

Her desire to live her life alone without the love of a man had changed. She would forever mourn the death of her brother, but she realized now she still had the capacity to love, and love deeply.

Somehow Dallas had gotten through her self-defenses, had broken down the walls she'd tried to erect around herself after Zeke's death. And she wasn't happy about it. She wasn't happy at all.

This had heartbreak written all over it, and for the life of her she couldn't see how to prevent it from happening. She didn't believe in fairy tales, and even if she did, Dallas had already had his with his wife, and he had made it clear to her that he wasn't looking for another one.

Despite his desire for her, Avery hadn't missed the love that had been in Dallas's voice when he'd spoken of Ivy. As much as she had fallen in love with him, he'd given her absolutely no indication he'd ever change his mind about his own solitary future.

There had been no more kisses between them, nothing physical at all, although there were times she thought she felt his desire for her palpitating in the air.

But desire didn't necessarily have anything to do with love and it was obvious she couldn't make him love her enough to want to be a husband to her, and that broke her heart more than a little bit.

She returned to the living room and sat on the sofa as Dallas came back in. "Well, that was frustrating," she said of Chief Thompson's visit.

He sank down next to her. "Yeah, it was. I can't believe all the thugs in this town can manage to threaten you and get away with it."

"I can't believe they're smart enough to have alibis that law enforcement can't break," she replied.

"Sooner or later something will break," he replied. "One of them will make a mistake or brag to the wrong person. We just need to be patient."

She was running out of patience. How long could they continue with Dallas staying here as her bodyguard? The real question was how long could she continue to have him in the house and not confess to him how she really felt about him?

The problem was she had yet to learn anything about him that would make her not love him. He picked up after himself and was always pleasant and helpful. There had to be a chink in his armor, and suddenly it seemed vital that she find it.

"I don't feel like cooking tonight," she said.

"That's not a problem. I'll take care of it," he replied easily.

"I'm not sure I'll like what you make." She curled up in the corner of the sofa and gazed at him.

He laughed. "Okay, then why don't you tell me what you'd like for me to make and I'll try to accommodate your taste buds."

His response irritated her because it was so darned nice. "What if I told you I think your cooking sucks?" she continued.

Once again he laughed. "Then I would suggest whenever you don't feel like cooking we either order in or we eat out. I certainly wouldn't want you to be forced to eat my cooking if you think it's bad."

"It's not bad. I just said that to see if I would make you mad."

He quirked an eyebrow upward. "Why would you want to make me mad?"

"I was just curious what kind of a temper you have," she replied.

"You should know by now that it takes a lot to make me angry."

"But I really don't know that," she protested. She got up from the sofa, feeling restless and on edge. "I feel like you've been on your very best behavior while you've been here."

He laughed yet again. "I can promise you I've been on my normal behavior."

"Stop laughing. I'm being serious here." She glared at him. Someplace inside she knew she was being unreasonable, but she needed…she *wanted* to be angry with him.

"Okay, then what is it you want to know?" The humor disappeared from his face.

"When you get angry, what do you do?" She hoped he'd tell her he screamed and cussed, that he punched and broke things.

He frowned. "I don't know, I guess it depends on why I'm angry." His eyes narrowed slightly. "What are you afraid of, Avery? That I'll get angry and beat my kids? Are you trying to make me angry right now?"

"Maybe…maybe I want to see how you act when you aren't on your best behavior."

"I could say the same about you," he countered. "Maybe you haven't been your real self since I've been here."

"I've totally been my real self. I'm too pregnant and too tired to be anything else." Once again she glared at him.

He cocked his head to one side and studied her for a long moment. "Is there a reason you're trying to pick a fight with me?"

Of course, that was exactly what she was trying to do. She wanted to pick a fight and get angry with him. She wanted him to do something or say something that would make her not like him as much… make her not love him at all.

However, as she stared at him, her eyes filled with

tears, and just that quickly her emotions spun out of control and she began to cry.

"Avery." Dallas got up from the sofa.

She halted him from coming any closer to her by holding up a hand. "I—I think maybe I need a nap," she finally managed to say, and then she ran down the hallway to her bedroom.

She cried for several minutes. Lulu hadn't even followed her back to the bedroom. The pooch had stayed with Dallas in the living room. The little traitor.

After a short period of time she was unsure what she was crying about. She'd survived fine before loving Dallas Colton and she would survive just fine after loving him. She'd do whatever was best for her children and that was that.

She finally fell asleep and awoke an hour later, feeling sheepish about what had happened with Dallas before she'd escaped to her room.

Getting out of bed, she then went into the bathroom to wash away any evidence of her tears. Finally, leaving her room, she realized she owed him an apology. She found him in the kitchen eating a ham and cheese sandwich. He offered her a tentative smile when she entered.

"Hi," she said, and sank down in the chair across from his.

"Feeling better?" he asked.

"Feeling remorseful about what happened before. I'm really sorry, Dallas. I don't know what got into me."

"It's okay," he replied easily. "You want a sandwich?" He started to get up.

"Sit tight, I've got it. Anything happen while I napped?" she asked, as she pulled the ham and cheese out of the fridge.

"Absolutely nothing," he replied.

She was grateful that as they ate lunch there was no more talk about her little breakdown.

It wasn't until later that evening that she felt the need to distance herself from him once again. At the moment they were seated side by side on the sofa, watching a goofy movie that didn't have the capacity to take her out of her own head.

"You're very quiet this evening. Are you feeling okay?" He broke the silence that had existed between them.

"I'm feeling fine and I'm just watching the movie," she replied. She frowned. "Actually, that's not exactly true. I was really thinking that maybe it was time to send you home."

One of his brows lifted as he gazed at her. "And what would make you think this? Am I driving you crazy?"

"No, silly," she replied. "You know you've been the perfect housemate."

"Then why are you trying to get rid of me?"

"I'm not trying to get rid of you. I've loved having you here." The problem was she'd loved it way too much. "But, Dallas, I need to be fair. It's been over two weeks and there have really been no more threats to me."

"What do you call what happened last night with Joel Asman?"

"What Chief Thompson called it. He was rattling my cage, but he didn't try to break in, didn't do anything to make me feel in imminent danger. It's been very selfish of me to keep you here. You have your work with the cowboys to get back to, your own life to live."

"Have you considered that maybe there haven't been any more threats against you because I am here? That maybe Asman didn't try anything last night because he knew I was here in the house?"

"Okay, so how do we know when there isn't any longer a threat? Do you just intend to live here forever?" Not that she wouldn't love that, but his presence had become a small form of torture. Each minute with him she fell a little more in love with him, and eventually she knew she wouldn't be able to keep her feelings for him inside. She would have to tell him how she felt.

"Let's give it another week or so. By that time maybe Chad or Danny will have heard something from their street snitches that will make us both feel better about things."

"I think I'll call Chad in the morning," she replied. "Maybe he'll tell us that Joel's appearance on the sidewalk was his swan song and the creeps have all moved on from me."

Dallas frowned. "I've never really understood what the end game was with these creeps."

"What do you mean? They want revenge because I put away Dwayne Conway."

"I would think they'd be threatening somebody in a case where their threats could make a difference. You aren't even working right now."

He shifted position and his frown grew deeper. "I mean, so far they've been pretty stupid in trash-talking around town, and then Asman showing his face here. If anything happens to you, he's made himself the number one suspect."

"Nobody ever said these guys were rocket scientists," she replied drily.

"As far as getting back to my own life, right now the safety of you and the babies is my life," he stated. "Unless my presence here is bothering you, don't worry about me. I'm right where I want to be."

She stifled a sigh and turned her gaze toward the television once again. If only he wanted to be here for her…aside from the babies she carried.

But she couldn't fool herself. He wasn't in love with her. He didn't want to build a future with her other than how they would interact as coparents.

Would another woman be able to change his mind about remarrying? Would another woman eventually be special enough for him to put his dead wife truly in his past, and make him look forward to a future with her?

Avery hoped so. If she couldn't have him, then she hoped he'd find love with somebody else. She wished that for him. She couldn't imagine that for the rest of his life he'd really be happy with only the ghost of a woman to keep him company.

"Avery, face it. You're stuck with me for a while longer," he finally said.

He offered her the heart-stopping smile that sent warm flutters throughout her being. She returned his smile, but knew she needed to spend the next week or so figuring out how to fall out of love with the father of her children.

Chapter 11

It had been three days since Chief Thompson stopped by to give them an update. During that time Avery had seemed preoccupied and a bit distant. And if she wasn't being distant she often appeared to be on the verge of tears.

And he absolutely hated to see her cry.

Dallas had racked his brain, trying to think if it was possible he'd done anything to upset her, but he couldn't think of a single thing.

He finally decided maybe it had something to do with her pregnancy. Her due date was approaching and maybe that had her preoccupied and emotional. He certainly didn't pretend to know how a pregnant woman felt as her time to deliver grew near.

For all he knew the way she was acting was perfectly normal.

He definitely knew she was uncomfortable. Each evening when they settled on the sofa, it took her several minutes to find a good position. Her belly seemed to have grown even bigger in the last few days.

So he knew she was ill at ease, but maybe she was upset because she hadn't been able to really nest in the way she'd described to him. She wasn't getting much extra sleep that he could tell, and she hadn't even indulged herself in her olive and potato chip snacks.

"Do you want more toast?" Her voice pulled him from his thoughts and back to breakfast.

"No, thanks, I'm good." He took a sip of his coffee and then set the cup down. "I was just thinking that if you want to make an appointment to get your toenails and fingernails done, then I'll be glad to take you and sit with you. I know that's something you wanted to do before the babies arrive."

She stared at him for a long moment, her eyes wide and suddenly shimmering with tears. "Thank you."

"Avery, what's wrong?" he asked in concern as she dabbed her eyes with her napkin.

She waved her hand as if to dismiss him, then released a laughing sob. "Don't you worry about me. My hormones are just crazy right now. If you really don't mind, then I'll make an appointment at my nail salon for tomorrow or the next day."

"That would be fine," he assured her. "Now, is there something I can do to help your hormone issue?"

She laughed. "No, but thanks for asking." She sobered quickly and stood and began to clear the dishes. "Once I'm done here I'm going to spend some more time on the computer."

There was that distance again. He heard it in her voice. By the time he finished the last of his coffee she was already out of the kitchen. Maybe she was tired of his presence in the house. Maybe she was beginning to start to feel that he was an intrusion. She'd certainly seemed like she was trying to get rid of him, judging by some of their conversations over the past three days.

He was torn. He didn't want to leave her defenseless to the kind of person who had tormented Lulu and written that threatening note. He didn't want to take a chance that somebody was lurking around in the shadows just waiting for him to leave so they could strike at her. And that's why he was reluctant to leave her house, reluctant to leave her.

He finally set his computer up on the table and hoped that thinking about a serial killer would wipe thoughts and worries about Avery out of his mind.

They had been working for about an hour when Avery called him to the living room. "I found a familiar name," she said. "Corgan, Horace Corgan. Apparently, he was dishonorably discharged from the army thirty-nine years ago. Who exactly is he?"

"If I remember right, he's a cousin to Elliot and Adam." Dallas frowned thoughtfully. Adam was a respected rancher and Elliot had died in prison after being convicted of the murders of young women that had rocked the small town forty years ago.

"Horace would have army buttons, wouldn't he?" Avery asked.

"Yeah, I would think he would," Dallas replied.

"Is it possible he's some sort of a copycat who is killing people now?"

"At this point I think anything is possible." He stared at the name. "I don't think anyone thought about Horace. He might have been interviewed initially, but I wonder if he was fully investigated."

"When Elliot was arrested I'm sure nobody else was investigated," she said. "Everyone believed Elliot was guilty."

"I need to call Forrest and let him know what you've found. I also need to let Chief Thompson know." Dallas went back in the kitchen to make the calls.

"Horace Corgan…" Chief Thompson repeated the name after Dallas mentioned it. "He's definitely flown under our radar. And you say he was dishonorably discharged from the army?"

"Yeah. He would have had army buttons, Chief."

"I'll be damned," Archer said softly. "How did we miss this? Let me do a little research and see where he's living now. I'll get right back to you."

Dallas didn't have long to wait. Archer called back within minutes with the location. "If it's possible I'd like you and Forrest to handle interviewing him. Hopefully, it can be done tomorrow, but I've got my hands full here and can't get away."

"No problem. I'll talk to Forrest and we'll get it done."

"Good, I'll text both of you the actual address. We'll see what Horace can add to the conversation."

They clicked off and then Dallas phoned his brother to make their plans. When the calls were completed, he returned to the living room, where Avery had moved to sit on the sofa.

"How do you feel about a ride to Austin in the morning?" he asked.

"What's in Austin?"

"Horace Corgan. Chief Thompson is good with Forrest and Rae and you and me going to talk to him. According to Chief Thompson Horace is in bad health. If he's responsible for these latest murders, maybe he'll want to clear his conscience."

"Wouldn't that be nice," she replied. "I'm definitely in."

"It's a bit of a long drive. Are you sure you're up to that kind of a car ride?"

"If Horace Corgan has some answers that might help, then I'm not about to miss out on hearing them," she replied firmly. "I can sit in a car just fine."

"I was also wondering if you feel up to an evening out?" he asked.

She looked at him cautiously. "Out where?"

"I thought we'd go out to dinner at the diner. I'd like to see what kind of gossip I can learn about Horace, and there's always some old-timers who eat there almost every night."

He saw the faint edge of fear that leaped into the depths of her green eyes. She might talk a good game about him returning to his own life. She might want to convince herself that the danger to her was gone. But that darkening of her eyes told him she wasn't quite there yet. He wondered now if fear was what had kept her from making a nail appointment before now.

"Avery, I will do everything in my power to keep you safe, but I'll understand if you don't want to go."

Her chin shot up and the fear in her eyes vanished beneath a steely strength. "I refuse to be a prisoner in my own house. I would love to have dinner with you at the diner this evening."

It was at that moment, with her eyes blazing with an inner strength, that he realized much to his dismay that she was exactly the kind of woman he could fall in love with…if he was really looking to fall in love again. Which he wasn't…

This was the first time they'd be out of the house since Joel Asman had stood on the sidewalk and stared at her place with such malevolence it had iced her insides.

Just after five, they left the house for the diner. Thankfully, there was nobody lurking around and they didn't appear to be followed.

She was clad in a light green blouse that she knew complimented her eyes and brown maternity slacks. She'd taken extra care with her makeup and hair, not so much for Dallas, but rather for herself. She wanted to show everyone in town she wasn't afraid, that the bad guys weren't winning and didn't have her cowering in fear.

Still, it was always a little nerve-racking in the initial moments when they left the house to get into his truck in the driveway.

Once they were safely in his vehicle and on their way, she began to relax. "I have to admit it feels nice to be out of the house."

"Tonight we're on a mission, not only to eat a nice meal out, but also to gather as much information as we can about Horace Corgan."

"We could break the case tomorrow," she said optimistically.

"Wouldn't that be nice, but I'm not going to hold my breath." He angled into a parking space and cut the engine. He unfastened his seat belt and then turned to face her. "Avery, if anyone or anything inside the diner makes you feel unsafe, just tell me. I'll whisk you back home in the blink of an eye."

"Dallas, as long as I'm in your company I feel perfectly safe," she replied. "Now, let's get inside and see what we can find out. Besides, as usual the twins are hungry."

They walked in and immediately Dallas leaned into her. "There's the man I was hoping would be here tonight." He gestured toward a small, thin man seated alone in a booth.

Avery immediately recognized him: George Severnson, a ninety-four-year-old widower who could still fiddle with the best of them and was the oldest resident in town.

They made their way to his booth. "Hey, George, mind if we join you?" Dallas asked.

George's blue eyes crinkled at the corners as he offered them a toothless grin. "Ain't often anyone wants to sit with an old geezer like me."

"Actually, we'd like to ask you some questions," Dallas said.

"Sit and ask away." He pointed to the seat opposite him.

Avery and Dallas had just slid into the booth when the waitress appeared to take their orders. Avery ordered the meat loaf special, Dallas got a bacon cheeseburger and George opted for a plate of spaghetti.

"George, your dinner is on me tonight," Dallas said.

"Well, if that's the case add on a piece of that

caramel apple pie that I like so much," George replied. "Hell, add on two pieces. I'll take one home," he told the waitress. He then looked from Dallas to Avery. "Must be some important questions you want to ask me if you're bribing me with a free dinner."

"We'll get to those in a minute," Dallas replied. "Are you still fiddling?"

The old man's pale blue eyes lit up once again. "Every chance I get," he declared. "In fact, I just won first place in a talent contest over at the Elks' Club the other night."

"Good for you," Dallas said.

As the two men shared a conversation about fiddling, Avery gazed around, checking out the other diners, making sure that none of Dwayne Conway's "friends" were in the restaurant.

Thankfully, she didn't see any of them. They were probably in a dank dark cave somewhere, plotting her demise, she thought darkly.

She suddenly realized George was looking at her expectantly. "I'm sorry?"

"Your man here just told me you're carrying his twins. What a blessing that is," George said.

"Thank you." She smiled, although she wondered if she should try to explain to George that Dallas wasn't her man. She decided not to say anything. Besides, her relationship with Dallas was far too complicated for her to even think about at the moment.

"My wife, God rest her soul, couldn't give me any

210 Colton 911: Target in Jeopardy

children," George said. "But I loved that woman with all my heart and soul." For a moment the slight man appeared even older than he was as sadness swept over his wrinkled features.

He straightened his shoulders and the sadness fell away. "But that was then and this is now, and I love my fiddle and that caramel apple pie."

Just then their food was delivered. "So, what did you want to ask this old man?" George sucked in a long strand of spaghetti, the end whipping his cheek with a bit of sauce. He used the back of his sleeve to wipe it away.

"We were wondering what you might know about Horace Corgan," Dallas said.

"Good Lord, now that's a name from the past." George looked at them in surprise. "What on earth would you want to know about that man?"

"Anything you can tell us about him," Avery said. "It's really important, George."

He frowned. "I don't know a lot about him. We didn't really run in the same circles. I do know he and Beau Lemmon were fairly tight." George frowned. "Has there been any word on who killed Beau? Is that what this is about?"

"Unfortunately, no," Dallas replied. "We still don't know who murdered him."

Beau Lemmon was Rae Lemmon's father, and Rae and Forrest had recently fallen in love. Rae had been devastated when Beau had been found in a grave on her property. Thankfully, Forrest had been there to help her through her grief. But Beau had been murdered, and so far there had been no clues as to who was responsible for his death.

George shook his head and slurped in another mouthful of spaghetti. "Strange things going on in this town. You think Horace is responsible for Beau's death?"

"We don't know if Horace is responsible for anything yet. We just wanted to get a general idea of what kind of man he was," Dallas replied.

"You know he got a dishonorable discharge from the army. I don't know the details, but I wouldn't be surprised if it wasn't about him flirting with the women. Horace definitely liked the young ladies," George said with a shake of his head.

"It's not against the law to like young ladies," Avery said an hour later, when she and Dallas were headed back to her house.

"True, but I still look forward to speaking with Horace tomorrow."

"What time are we leaving?"

"Forrest and Rae are picking us up around nine." Dallas parked in Avery's driveway and she waited for him to come around to get her. He threw a protective arm around her shoulders as they walked to the front door.

Once inside, they sat on the sofa. "You know it's

very possible Horace has nothing to do with any of this," she said.

"True, but he would have army buttons in his possession, and we know buttons were found at several of the murder scenes. At the very least maybe we'll be able to take him off the suspect list for good. He was only interviewed once early on in the case. In any case he needs to be interviewed again."

For the next half an hour they talked about the case and then, even though it was still relatively early, Avery decided to call it a night.

It was getting incredibly difficult for her to find a comfortable position in bed or anywhere else. She was definitely looking forward to the birth of her babies more and more each day. She couldn't wait to get them out of her body and into her arms.

She climbed into bed and stared up at the ceiling. It was in the utter quiet of the night that her mind was the most chaotic. And all the chaos was about Dallas and her feelings for him.

Despite everything that had to do with good sense and rational thought, she wished he was in bed with her right now. She wished he had his arms wrapped tightly around her and she could feel his heart beating against her own.

But she had to be smart about things. A good relationship with Dallas was the very best gift she could give her babies, and she couldn't, absolutely wouldn't allow her emotions to get in the way of that.

Eventually the threat against her would be re-solved and he would move back to his cabin. She would probably see him only when he picked up the twins and brought them back. Despite her physical discomfort, she shoved all the thoughts out of her head and closed her eyes. Then she finally drifted off to sleep.

Dallas's arms were tight around her as they gazed into first one crib and then the other. The twins cooed, a chorus of health and happiness.

He turned her around and gazed deeply into her eyes. "I love you, Avery." As his words warmed her, his lips took hers in a fiery kiss that weakened her knees.

Then they were in her bed, making love with all the passion, all the love they felt for each other. Avery clung to him, certain of her future, of their future together. It was the fairy tale she'd been afraid to hope for, the happy ending she now believed in.

And then she was running. She raced down first one dark street and then another. Behind her Joel Asman and Max Malone chased after her, each of them wielding huge knives that shone in the moon-light.

Her breaths came in short, painful pants as she kept one arm wrapped around her pregnant belly. "Dallas!" She screamed his name over and over again as the two men behind her drew closer and closer.

But her cries for help echoed down the dark streets and nobody seemed to hear them. Tears half blinded her as she realized the thugs were going to catch her. They were going to kill her, and with her death, her babies would die.

"Dallas," she screamed once again in a final plea for help.

"Avery, wake up. Honey, you're having a nightmare."

Dallas's deep voice penetrated through her layers of sleep and vanquished the nightmare. She opened her eyes, sat up and wrapped her arms tightly around his neck as sobs escaped her.

"You're okay. Avery, you're safe." He rubbed his hands up and down her back as she buried her face in the crook of his neck.

"Th-they were chasing me with knives. J-Joel and Max. Th-they were going to k-kill me."

"Nobody is going to kill you, Avery. It was just a bad dream."

Slowly she managed to get her tears under control. She released her hold on him. "I'm sorry, Dallas. I didn't mean to wake you."

He smiled and used his thumbs to gently wipe the tears off her cheeks. "Wake me? Hell, you scared me half to death. I heard you screaming my name and I thought when I came in here you'd be in the middle of birthing those babies right here in the bed."

"No birth. I just thought for sure I was going to be killed." Even though she was now fully awake, the terror of the nightmare still coursed through her. "I'm sorry for waking you and scaring the hell out of you."

"Are you okay to go back to sleep?"

She started to nod that she was, but then stopped. "I know it's a lot to ask, but would you consider sleeping in here with me for the rest of the night?"

"I can do that," he agreed immediately. She scooted over to allow him room to slide beneath the sheet next to her.

He was clad only in boxers and as he gathered her into his arms, his bare skin warmed her. There was nothing sexual about it; his embrace comforted her and gave her a sense of security as she drifted off to sleep once again.

By the time she awakened the next morning, she was once again alone in the bed. However, the sheets still held the warmth of his body heat, letting her know it hadn't been long since he'd left.

Thankfully nothing was awkward as they ate breakfast and prepared for the day's travel. It was approximately one hundred and ninety miles to Austin. Seven hours in the car would make a very long day for her in her condition, but she wasn't about to sit this one out.

Even though she wasn't working right now that didn't mean she wasn't interested in the crime taking place in town, and she was particularly interested in the mummy murders.

At a quarter to nine she and Dallas were in the living room waiting for Forrest and Rae to arrive.

"I can't wait for a chance to visit with Rae," she said, petting Lulu, who was seated in her lap. "I want to hear all about her giving birth to little Connor and what it's like to have a three-month-old."

"Whatever she tells you, for you it will be times two," Dallas replied with a warm grin.

"I'm sure we'll muddle through with two." A car honked outside.

"That must be them," Dallas said. Avery placed Lulu on the floor, grabbed her purse and followed him out the door. Forrest and Dallas sat in the front seats and Avery sat in the back seat with Rae.

Rae was an attractive brunette who worked as a paralegal at the local offices of Lucas, Jolley and Fitzsimmons. She was bright and friendly, and for most of the drive to Austin the two women chattered about birth and the challenges of parenthood.

"I'll warn you, Dallas, don't take personally anything she says to you while she's in labor," Rae said. "It's possible she'll curse you and she'll want to do bodily harm to you."

They all laughed. "I'm sure I can take whatever she dishes out," Dallas replied.

"Have you two been to all the birthing classes?" Rae asked.

Dallas whirled around and looked at Avery with panic. "Birthing classes? Were we supposed to go to those?"

"With everything that's been going on, there really hasn't been time," Avery replied.

"All you need to remember, Dallas, is to remind Avery to breathe through the labor pains," Rae said.

"Okay, I can do that," he replied.

"How about a pit stop," Rae suggested, when they were about halfway to Austin. "I'm sure Avery could use a bit of a stretch and so could I."

Avery smiled at her gratefully. They made the pit stop where the other three fueled up on coffee and Avery got a bottle of water and a chocolate-covered doughnut, and then blamed it on the twins for loving chocolate.

However, the closer they got to Austin, the more the air in the car grew palpable with tension. Forrest, as a working law enforcement agent, had to be thinking about the interview they would have with Horace. She was sure Dallas was thinking similar thoughts.

Not only did Horace have the same kind of forty-year-old army buttons that had been found near the victims' bodies, he was also the cousin of the man who had died in prison for the crime of killing seven women.

Was it possible Horace had killed the recent victims? Was it possible he'd been part of his cousin's killing spree all those years ago? There were so many questions, and hopefully after today they would finally have some answers.

"Okay, we're almost there. I want to talk about this case so we're all on the same page when we go in to speak with Horace," Forrest said.

"It all started when Maggie Reeves found the skeleton on the Live Oak Ranch property after the hurricane," Dallas said. "It was the seventh girl who was murdered forty years ago," Dallas replied.

"And that skeleton was Emmeline Thompson, Chief Thompson's little sister," Rae said. "Then Patrice Eccleston's body was discovered in the Lone Star Pharma parking lot and the mummified body was found in my backyard. And then my dad was murdered." Rae's voice thickened with emotion, and Avery reached over and gave her hand a reassuring squeeze.

"And we're going to find the person responsible for his murder, Rae," Forrest exclaimed firmly.

"We all know that Elliot Corgan went to prison for the murder of the women and then he committed suicide, but now I have to wonder if he was really guilty," Dallas said.

"There was definitely some question at the time about Elliot's suicide," Forrest added.

Everyone fell silent. They got off the highway in Austin and eventually turned down a tree-lined street of small houses with neat front yards. "It should be up ahead on the right," Forrest said.

He passed two more houses and then pulled

into the driveway of a weathered white house with black shutters. Avery desperately hoped they would find some answers inside. Right now Horace was their best hope for solving the murders that haunted Whisperwood.

Chapter 12

Dallas had no idea what to expect when he knocked on Horace Corgan's front door, but he certainly hadn't expected to be greeted by a uniformed nurse.

The middle-aged woman wore a name tag that identified her as Jane Oliver. It wasn't until Forrest showed her his badge that she allowed them all to step into the small living room.

Although the room appeared neat and clean, the smell of sickness hung heavy in the air.

"We need to speak with Horace," Forrest said to Jane, who immediately frowned in disapproval.

"Mr. Corgan is quite ill," she said.

"Is he able to speak?" Forrest asked.

"Well, yes," she replied.

"We just need to ask him a few questions," Dallas said.

"I hope you don't plan on taxing him," she replied. "He tires quite easily."

Dallas exchanged a quick glance with his brother. Nobody had told them that Horace was ill. "How sick is he?" Dallas asked.

"Mr. Corgan has stage four lung cancer. His health has gone downhill dramatically in the past couple of weeks and recently he was placed on oxygen full-time. He's also trying to gain some strength back after a recent heart attack," the nurse explained. "He's quite ill."

"We still need to talk to him," Forrest replied firmly.

Dallas was glad his brother was so determined. They hadn't driven all this way to be turned away by an overprotective nurse.

Jane's features tightened in obvious disapproval once again. "Follow me," she said curtly.

She led them down a short hallway to a small bedroom, where the old man was in bed and hooked up to all kinds of machines.

"These people are here to talk to you, Mr. Corgan." Jane moved to stand at the head of the bed, where a blue computer monitor displayed his vitals.

Horace looked like a dying man. His skeletal body was scarcely visible beneath the light blue bedsheets. His wheezing breaths filled the air, along with the click and whirr of the various machines. His skin tone was the pasty gray of impending death.

Forrest introduced himself and the others, and Horace grinned. "I don't get many visitors. To what do I owe this pleasure?" He turned and looked at Jane. "Prop me up."

She rearranged the pillows behind him so that he was sitting up a little more.

"We have some questions to ask you, Mr. Corgan," Forrest said.

"Questions about what? And call me Horace. You don't need to be formal with me."

"We understand you were once in the army," Dallas said.

"That was a hell of a long time ago," Horace replied.

"We also understand you once lived in Whisperwood," Forrest said.

"That's right."

"Did you keep your army buttons?" Dallas asked.

"I did, until I started losing them here and there. But I'm sure you aren't here to talk to me about some old buttons."

"Actually, we're here about some murders that happened in Whisperwood about forty years ago, and murders that are happening right now," Dallas said.

Horace laughed, but the laughter turned into a fit of violent coughing. "I was wondering when or if anyone would get around to talking to me," he finally managed to gasp.

"We're here now to talk to you," Forrest said.

"What do you want to know? If I killed those women? I'll confess when I was younger I had an appetite for the young beauties."

He paused and his gaze grew distant. A smile curved his lips, a smile that completely creeped Dallas out. He glanced over to Avery, who looked as uncomfortable as he felt.

The old man focused on them all once again. "I managed to escape the law, but dammit, it appears that there's no way I'm going to escape the devil, who is ready to take me way sooner than I wanted."

"We're sorry about your health," Forrest said. "But we need some answers, Horace."

He didn't acknowledge Forrest's statement, but remained silent for several long moments. "Sweet little Emmeline," he finally said. For a moment his breathing grew louder in the room. Again his gaze grew distant, as if he'd drifted back into the distant past.

Nobody else spoke. It was as if everyone but Horace was holding their breath, waiting to hear what the old man would say next. But the minute Horace had spoken the name of Chief Thompson's little sister, one of the victims, Dallas's tension had shot through the ceiling.

"She was a torment to me, that one with her pretty face and fetching ways. But she wasn't interested in me. Still, I'd decided I had to have her one way or the other and I did." His eyes gleamed with a sick light. "I suppose I can admit it now. I had her every way I wanted her and then I killed her. To preserve her beauty, I mummified her before I buried her."

Nurse Jane released a small gasp as she stepped back from the bed and stared at her patient. Dallas heard Avery gasp, too, and he gazed at her to make sure she was okay. The last thing he wanted was for her to get so upset she somehow was triggered into an early delivery.

"You okay?" he asked softly. She nodded.

Dallas was shocked by what Horace had just done. He'd confessed to raping and murdering Chief Thompson's little sister.

"What about the other six women?" Forrest asked. Once again the air in the room became charged with a tense anticipation.

Horace cast him a sly smile. "Didn't you hear the news? My cousin Elliot went to prison for those murders." He laughed again, then once more went into a choking spasm that went on for several long minutes. When he was finally finished, Nurse Jane handed him a tissue to wipe away the blood he'd coughed up.

"Elliot was the perfect patsy," he finally said. "That man couldn't keep his mouth shut long enough to stay out of prison. He spewed all his women-hating ways to anyone who would listen, and made himself the number one suspect in those murder cases."

Horace's smile fell away and his skeletal features twisted into a scowl. "But then I heard he was looking for an appeal, and he had a lawyer who was interested in taking the case. Elliot intended to tell everything he knew. And he knew way too much. He was going to put my name in the picture and that's the last thing I wanted."

"We heard he committed suicide in prison…that he hanged himself in his cell," Dallas said. He was astonished by what the man had already admitted He'd confessed that he'd raped and killed Emmeline. One murder mystery solved. What next?

Horace barked a laugh. "Elliot was too much of a wimp to commit suicide. It's amazing what you can get an inmate who is never getting out of prison to do if you just add a little money to his books."

"So somebody helped Elliot to his death. It wasn't a suicide," Forrest asked.

"That's right." Again Horace smiled, that sly grin that Dallas found so disturbing.

"So, who killed those six other women forty years ago?" Dallas asked. "Was it Elliot or was it you?"

Horace's smile widened, stretching his thin lips into a grin that turned his skeletal features into a death mask. "They were all my beauties, so sweet and so pretty. I just couldn't help myself. I had them all and when I was finished with them, I buried them."

Murder mystery solved. Dallas stared at the old man who had been responsible for seven young women's deaths. "Why are you confessing to all this now?" he asked.

"What do I have to lose? What are you going to do? Throw an old, dying man in prison? If that's where I wind up, at least I'll have a bed and three squares a day for the rest of my life. I'll be placed in the hospital ward, where I'll have everything I need and nobody will be able to bother me."

"What about the mummified remains that were found on my property," Rae asked. "Do you know anything about her?"

Horace's eyes half closed, as if he was once again drifting back to the past. "Ah, sweet Leora." His eyes fluttered and then closed, and his breathing grew louder and quickened.

"Leora who?" Rae asked.

"Leora Sweeney," Horace replied, and opened his eyes. "She was Emmeline's best friend. Such a beautiful young woman. Of course I had to have her, too."

"And what about my father? Did you kill him?" Rae asked softly, her grief audible in her voice.

"Who in the hell is your father?" Horace asked.

"Beau... Beau Lemmons," Forrest said, and pulled Rae closer to his side.

"Nah, I didn't do him." Once again the sick man went into a coughing spell that left him gasping.

"Just breathe through your nose," the nurse said. "Breathe in the oxygen, Horace."

Horace nodded and leaned his head back as he did

what she told him. "Are we done here?" he asked, when he'd finally caught his breath.

"Just one more question," Forrest said. "Did you kill Patrice Eccleston?"

Horace frowned. "No, I never heard of her."

Dallas looked at Forrest. "Maybe we should step outside and have a discussion." He wanted to make sure they had asked the man all the questions they needed to.

"Yes, you all have overtaxed Mr. Corgan," Jane said, the disapproval back in her voice.

The four of them moved out of the bedroom and back into the living room. "Wow," Avery said. "I can't believe he just confessed to so much."

"He's got nothing much to lose now. He does look sick, but I'd like to take a look at his medical records to see if maybe he's still in some way playing us all," Forrest replied.

Dallas looked at his brother curiously. "What are you thinking?"

"Maybe he's banking on the sympathy vote from us. Maybe he isn't as close to death as he's pretending to be, and he's banking on us not turning in a dying man."

"But he couldn't have known we were coming today," Avery said. "I saw the blood he coughed up. He definitely looks like a dying man."

Forrest frowned and released a deep breath. "You're right. I'm not thinking straight. My head is spinning with everything he told us. All I know is that he's one evil son of a bitch."

"He is that," Dallas agreed. "So, can anyone think of any more questions we need to ask him before we leave here?"

"I think we definitely got more answers than we expected," Forrest said drily. "Poor Elliot got the rap for his cousin's crimes and then was strung up and murdered." He shook his head.

Jane joined them in the living room. She had to be in shock, given what she'd just heard about her patient. "He's sleeping," she said to nobody in particular.

"I need to call Chief Thompson and see how he wants us to proceed," Forrest said. "I'm sure he'll want to coordinate with the local authorities here."

"At least he has his answer as to who killed his sister. Maybe that will finally bring him some closure," Avery said.

"Still, we don't know who killed Beau and Patrice," Dallas said. "I'm pretty sure if Horace was responsible for those deaths, he would have told us." One murderer had been found, but another one still walked the streets of his town.

Forrest pulled out his cell phone, but before he could make the call, from the bedroom came the sound of Horace coughing hysterically. His coughs sounded violent.

The nurse rushed into the room and the four of

them followed on her heels. The oxygen tube was out, and it was obvious he was in great distress. The gray of his face had taken on a bluish tint. His hands appeared to be somehow tangled beneath the sheet and one of the machines began to squeal with an alarm sound.

Suddenly he stopped coughing. "Melody," he managed to whisper, and then his eyes rolled into the back of his head and the alarm sound changed to one of no pulse, no blood pressure.

Horace Corgan was dead.

It was almost midnight when Forrest dropped Avery and Dallas back at her house. Despite the lateness of the hour, the aching of her body and the shocking events of the long day, adrenaline still flooded through Avery.

The mummy killer was finally identified and now was dead. That should have been the end of things, but Horace's sudden death had certainly been more than suspicious. Not only was it odd that his oxygen tube had been removed prior to his death, but also it was discovered that his hands had been bound beneath the sheet.

And who the heck was Melody? The name had been the last word Horace had spoken before death had taken him. But none of them knew of a Melody.

"What a day," Avery said as she collapsed on the sofa. Lulu immediately jumped into her lap.

"It was a really long day for you. How are you feeling?" Dallas asked, sinking down next to her.

"Like I should be exhausted, but I'm not. I'm a bit sore from the drive, but it's nothing serious. It was such a strange and horrible day." She'd listened to a man confess to killing so many young women, and then she'd watched him die under mysterious circumstances.

"At least he managed to solve a lot of murder cases, but his death was definitely strange. It looked like a murder to me." Dallas frowned.

"The window in his bedroom was cracked open and there was no screen on it. I guess it's possible somebody got inside, tied his hands and pulled out his oxygen tube, and then left while we were all talking in the living room," she replied. It had definitely been more than suspicious.

"But despite all the emergency and police officers that responded at the house, Nurse Jane Oliver managed to slip away. She either killed him or she knows something about his death." Dallas's frown deepened.

It had all definitely been disturbing. The Austin authorities had questioned the four of them at length and had finally let them go. Had it been the nurse who had yanked the oxygen away from Horace and then bound his hands, to make it impossible for him to save himself?

"Hopefully, the authorities will be able to find and

question her," Avery replied, and then stifled a yawn. "At least the mummy murders from all those years ago have been solved." The adrenaline that had filled her began to seep away. "I'm going to call it a night. Suddenly I'm exhausted." She placed Lulu on the floor and then pulled herself up from the sofa. Dallas got up, as well.

"I hope you sleep extra late tomorrow," he said, as he walked with her down the hall. "I know it's been a really long day for you."

They reached her door and she turned to face him. To her surprise he leaned in and captured her lips in a soft kiss that sent a sweet wave of heat fluttering into her heart.

He stepped back from her and smiled—the smile that still had the capacity to intensify the heat inside her, but now also created a hint of heartache.

"Good night, Avery," he said softly, and then turned and headed back down the hallway.

Avery and Lulu went into her room and she closed the door. Within minutes she was in bed and trying to quiet the chaos in her mind that the end of day always brought.

She finally drifted off to sleep, and awakened the next day shocked to realize it was almost eleven. She showered and dressed and went to find Dallas, who was sitting on the sofa with the television on. Lulu was curled up at his side and she realized at some point during the morning he must have opened her door to let the pooch out.

"Hey, sleepyhead," he greeted her.

"Hey yourself," she replied. "What are you watching?"

"All the news about the mummy killer being identified. We've gone national with the story. You just missed Chief Thompson giving a news conference."

"Let me get a cup of tea and then you can catch me up on everything."

She went into the kitchen and fixed her tea and then joined him on the sofa. "So, what have I missed?"

"Not much, since you were there in person for most of it. The main thing is Jane Oliver seems to still be missing and the authorities want to find her for questioning."

"More than a little bit suspicious," Avery murmured. She took a sip of tea and placed the cup on the coffee table in front of them. "But if she was responsible for his death, did she have some other motivation, or was it just because she'd heard what he did?"

"That's a mystery the authorities will have to solve. At least we don't have to chase down soldiers anymore. So maybe you should call and see if you can get into your nail place later today."

"I could just do a walk-in. I really don't need an appointment. I would like to have them done before the babies come. I have a feeling there won't be much time for myself once they arrive."

He smiled. "Then you just set the time and I'll be glad to take you."

"Thanks, Dallas. I really appreciate it." She turned her attention to the television, because she was afraid if she looked at him for one more minute, she might blurt out how much she was in love with him.

She wasn't sure how long she would be able to spend her days and nights with him before she spoke of her love, and she knew that would ruin everything.

She had to think of her babies first. The last thing she wanted to do was mess up her relationship with their father. She didn't want awkward handoffs and tense interaction with him in the future.

At two o'clock they left the house. As usual, Dallas watched his rearview mirror as they pulled out on the street and headed for Natalie's Nails.

"Do you really think the danger to me is still present?" she asked.

"I don't know," he said, after a moment of hesitation. "But I do know I'm not ready yet to leave that to chance. Are you?"

She placed a hand on her stomach, reminding herself that it wasn't just her own safety at risk, but also the babies she carried. "I guess not," she admitted.

She was just going to have to keep her feelings for him stuffed inside, no matter how difficult it was for her. At least for the next hour or so she could focus on being pampered as she got her nails done.

Natalie's Nails was like an oasis in the middle of

a desert. Palm trees and blue water were painted on the walls and several fountains filled the air with the sound of gurgling water. The setting was definitely tranquil despite the smells of acetone and other chemicals used to transform short, stubby nails into beautiful works of art.

As Maria, one of Natalie's nail specialists, filled the foot bowl with hot, sudsy water and eased Avery's feet in, she relaxed in the chair. Then Maria left them alone.

Dallas sat in the large, black leather massaging chair next to hers. "So, what exactly do they do for you when you get a pedicure?" he asked curiously.

"First you soak for a few minutes and then Maria will come back and scrub my feet with a brush. This exfoliates all the dead skin and feels absolutely wonderful. She then trims the nails and after that she rubs in all kinds of oils and lotions that make your feet feel wonderfully soft and rested. I've seen lots of men in here getting pedicures. You should get one."

"Nah," Dallas replied. "I'm good."

She grinned at him. "Come on, Dallas. In fact, I challenge you here and now to get your very first pedicure with me."

He glanced over at Maria and then looked back at Avery. "You're sure men do this?"

"Absolutely," she replied. "Are you up for it? Keep in mind I'm hugely pregnant with your children and you don't want to upset me."

"That's not playing fair," he replied with a laugh.

He reached down and pulled off one cowboy boot and then the other. "Okay, challenge accepted."

Avery motioned to Maria and within minutes Dallas had his own feet in a bowl of sudsy water. "I have to admit, this feels really good."

"If you want, you can turn on your chair massager, too." She watched as he looked down at the controls that would heat and beat, or roll in waves down his back.

He punched several of the buttons and then relaxed into the chair. "This feels great. I think maybe women have kept the salon a secret from men for too long."

She laughed, delighted that he was next to her. "You know, in some salons they have little fish in pools of water, and when you put your feet in they eat off the dead skin."

He leaped forward and raised his feet out of the bowl. "Is this one of the salons that do that?"

Once again she laughed, this time at the panicked look on his face. "No, I promise you there aren't any little critters in the water."

He eased his feet back down. "The only place I like to see fish is on the end of a pole or frying in my skillet."

"I'm assuming you intend to teach the kids to fish."

"And ride horses and learn to love the outdoors."

"I'd love that for them," Avery agreed. "I'd far rather see them be outdoorsy kids than cooped up inside with video games."

"That makes two of us. Still, I want them to be good students and learn good study habits."

Avery laughed. "They aren't even here yet and we're already worried about their study habits."

"I can't wait for them to get here." He held her gaze for a long moment and once again her love for him buoyed up inside her.

"I can't wait, either," she replied, grateful at that moment that Maria and another nail specialist came over to begin working on their feet.

It was obvious Dallas felt uncomfortable as the pedicure continued. The fact that he'd gone out of his comfort zone, that he'd agreed to it solely to please her, touched Avery in ways she'd never been touched before.

She chose a pretty pearly-pink polish for her toes and fingernails, while Dallas opted out of the polish process. An hour later they left the salon.

"Thank you for bringing me," she said, once they were in the truck and headed home.

"Thanks for introducing me to the joy of a pedicure. And if you tell anyone I got one, I'll have to kill you," he replied teasingly.

She laughed. "What a typical man."

They got back to the house and once again settled in on the sofa. "How about you rest for the remainder of the day and I'll take care of dinner tonight," he said.

"You aren't going to get an argument out of me," she replied.

At six o'clock they ate a meal of cheeseburgers and fries, and then settled once again on the sofa to await bedtime. Darkness fell outside as the night deepened. Once again as she sat next to him, her love for him so full in her chest, she was almost afraid to speak about anything.

Instead of allowing herself to talk about her feelings for him, she thought that maybe getting him to talk about the woman he'd been married to might confirm to her that Dallas would never, ever be hers.

Besides, she suddenly wanted to know more about the woman he'd committed his life to, and who Avery suspected still filled his heart to such a capacity that there wasn't room for another woman.

"Tell me about Ivy, Dallas," she said. She instantly felt his tension and wondered if she'd just made a big mistake.

Chapter 13

Dallas stared at Avery and waited for the stabbing, killing grief that always occurred when he thought of his dead wife. He waited and waited, and that stabbing pain didn't happen. Instead a hollow wind of loss swept through him. It was the sadness of having lost a loved one he would never forget, but it was a loss he could deal with.

"I'm sorry. I shouldn't have asked," Avery said hurriedly.

"No, it's okay." He leaned back against the sofa and for the first time since her death allowed memories of Ivy to fill his head. "She was beautiful and driven."

"How did you meet?"

"We actually met at the army recruitment office, where we both signed up for four years of duty." The memories continued to flood through him. "It was an instant connection and we wound up going out for coffee that day."

He got up from the sofa, needing to pace while he spoke of the wife he had lost. "She was bright and funny, and within three months we were married. And then we were deployed to different posts."

"That must have been hard on the two of you," Avery said.

"We managed the circumstances. We video chatted every day and tried to plan our leaves at the same time."

"Tell me more about what she was like as a person."

He turned and looked at Avery. It was funny how his memories of his dead wife were less sharp than they had once been. When he tried to bring up a vision of Ivy in his head, what he saw was Avery. When he thought about shared laughter it was always the laughter he shared with the twins' mother.

"Even though she had a good sense of humor, generally she was a serious woman who knew exactly what she wanted in her future. Her parents had divorced and her father disappeared from her life when she was six. Her mother struggled to make ends meet, and one of the reasons Ivy joined the army was for the educational opportunities that came with it. She wanted to make sure she always had the means to support herself and any children she might have."

"That's smart for any woman in this day and age," Avery replied.

He nodded. He walked over to the window and stared out into the night. He was still waiting for that familiar, agonizing grief to consume him. But it simply wasn't there. What he felt now was a profound sadness that she had died before her time and that they had never gotten to experience the many plans they had made for their lives.

Now those plans were gone, but life had handed him an unexpected gift and new plans for his future. Ivy was his past, an important part that he would never forget. He would always have love for her in his heart, but there was no place for her in his new future.

He turned back to look at Avery and was stunned to see tears trekking down her cheeks. "Avery! What's going on?" He walked over and sat next to her. "Why are you crying?"

She shook her head and swiped at the tears. "It's nothing," she replied, keeping her head down.

"Avery, look at me. It can't be nothing. 'Nothing' doesn't make you cry."

More tears chased each other down her cheeks. "It's foolish, really. I'll be fine in just a minute."

"But what started your tears?" he pressed.

She lowered her hands and looked up at him. Her

eyes were big and luminous and lovely. "I love you, okay? I love you, Dallas. I love you with all my heart and soul, and I want to spend all my days and nights with you." She clapped a hand over her mouth as he stared at her in utter surprise.

He hadn't expected this. Oh, he knew that she felt close to him, that she appreciated him watching over her and that she loved the kind of father she thought he was going to be.

But this…this declaration of love had him stunned.

Before he could reply, the back window exploded inward as a large rock flew through the glass and hit the floor.

"Stay here and lock the door after me," Dallas said urgently. He grabbed his gun off the coffee table and flew out the back door.

Every nerve in his body was electrified. It took a moment for his eyes to adjust to the darkness. Somebody had to be in her backyard to have thrown that large a rock through the window. He intended to catch the culprit. He had to catch the person and get him arrested.

There were plenty of trees and bushes to hide behind and he had no doubt that somebody was back there hiding. Where in the hell was he?

Dallas got a better grip on his gun as the coldness of a hunter overtook him. He sensed somebody close by. All he had to do was figure out where the thug was and what he intended to do next.

He hadn't taken the time to see if the rock had a message on it. He didn't give a damn about a message; he wanted the perp. He'd heard no rapid footsteps, no indication that whoever had thrown the rock had run away.

Approaching one of the bushes, he felt his muscles tense. The moonlight overhead was obscured by clouds, but there was enough illumination for him to see that nobody was there. So where was the bastard who had thrown the rock?

Before he could turn to check out the next bush, something crashed down on the back of his head. The blow exploded in his brain with flashing lights and he crumpled first to his knees and then to the ground.

His last conscious thought was that he now knew what the perp had wanted when he'd thrown that rock through the window. He'd wanted to get Dallas out of the house so he could get to Avery.

Avery! He screamed her name in his head and then darkness descended.

Where was Dallas? What was taking him so long? Avery stared at the big rock that had been propelled through the window. There was nothing written on it. There was no note attached. It was just an ordinary rock.

She stared at the back door worriedly. Where in the heck was Dallas? Why hadn't he come back in yet? She jumped as a knock sounded on her front door. Was that him?

She hurried over and peeked out the peep hole. It was Chad. What on earth was he doing here? She opened the door. "Chad, did you see Dallas anywhere?"

"Actually, I did. I just saw him running up the street. What's going on?"

She ushered him into the living room and pointed at the rock on the floor. "That just sailed through my window and Dallas went out to see if he could find who was responsible."

Chad frowned. "So, bad things are still happening? I came by to tell you that word on the street is the heat is completely off you, that Dwayne Conway's thug friends have found bigger and better targets."

"So then what's going on, and where is Dallas?" she asked frantically.

"Maybe Dallas will be back soon or maybe he'll never come back."

She looked at her friend in surprise. "Chad…why on earth would you say something like that?" She released an uneasy laugh. What was Chad doing here? How odd that he would show up right now.

"Does that make you afraid, Avery? To think that your bodyguard boyfriend might not return to protect you?"

Avery stared at him and her heart began to pound an unnatural rhythm. "Wha-what's going on, Chad?

Why have you come?" He had never stopped by at this time of the night before.

For the first time she noticed that his eyes were the cold, electric blue that she'd seen only when he was in the courtroom. There was absolutely no warmth in them.

A cord pulsed in the side of his neck and Lulu whined, as if responding to the sudden tension in the room. Avery bent down and took the dog into her arms. "What's going on, Chad?"

"I'll tell you what's going on, Avery. Poor Danny. You went and broke my buddy's heart."

"What are you talking about?" Avery asked, her heart now crashing into her ribs with a simmering panic. "How did I break his heart?" Dear Lord, where was Dallas? What had Chad done to him?

"You used him. You let him buy you diapers and put together cribs and believe he was going to be a part of your and your babies' lives. Then you threw him away when cowboy Colton rode back into the picture. You know who does things like that, Avery? A whore does things like that."

She blinked hard, shocked by his words. Whore? That was what the note around Lulu's neck had called her. Whore! "It was you all along," she said with a gasp, and took a step back from him.

"Yeah, it was me. You just tossed Danny away. Just like my wife, that whore, threw me away. You're just alike, the two of you. You use men and then trade them in for somebody you think might be better."

"That's not true. I'm not like that at all." She took another step back from him. "Chad, you know me. We're good friends. You and me and Danny…we're all good friends."

"We were good friends. We aren't anymore. You screwed it all up, Avery."

"What did you do to Dallas?" Her heart cried out Dallas's name as her fear grew to terror. She tasted her fear—an acidic, awful taste. It chilled her and goose bumps rose on her arms as the hair on the nape of her neck lifted.

"Don't worry about that Colton creep. He's just taking a nice, long nap."

"A nap? What do you mean?" Oh, God, what had Chad done to Dallas?

"I hit him over the head hard enough to put him into a nice long nap or maybe a coma. In either case he'll be out long enough for me to do what I need to do."

"And what is it you need to do?" she asked, nearly breathless with the terror that now exploded through her. The back of her throat had closed up with fear not only for herself and the babies, but for Dallas, as well.

Chad grinned, a half-mad grin Avery had never seen before. "You know Danny is like the little brother I never had. All I want is for him to be happy.

He is in love with you, Avery. He is in love with you and you broke his heart. If Danny can't have you and the babies, then nobody is going to." He pulled a knife from his pocket—what appeared to be a gleaming, wickedly sharp one.

As she realized his intentions, a scream escaped her and she turned and ran down the hallway. Chad followed right behind her, his footsteps hard and determined. She flew into her bedroom and slammed and locked the door.

Panic seared through her. Damn, damn. Her cell phone was in her purse in the living room. She couldn't call for help, and from what Chad had told her, she couldn't depend on Dallas coming to her rescue.

Oh please, God, don't let him be dead. How hard had he been hit? Hard enough to kill him? A sob choked her throat. The sob turned into a scream when Chad hit the door.

He laughed. "Do you really think a flimsy bedroom door lock is going to keep me out?" He hit the door again and it shuddered beneath the blow.

Oh God, it wasn't going to hold. She placed Lulu on the floor and ran to the side of her dresser. She had to somehow barricade the door.

She ignored the sudden tightness of her stomach and the pain that shot through her back. All she could focus on was her need to do something, anything, to stop Chad from getting into her bedroom.

She had to move the dresser in front of the door. At least that would create another barrier Chad would have to get through. Hopefully, it would be enough. It had to be enough to keep him from getting inside the room.

Sobbing, she pushed the side of the dresser with all her strength and managed to move it only about an inch. "Chad, please stop this now. I promise I won't tell anyone. Just go and we'll never mention this again."

"I'm not going anywhere except through this door."

"You're going to get caught if you don't leave now." She pushed on the dresser once again.

"How am I going to get caught? Chief Thompson and everyone else will believe your death was the result of a vendetta for putting Dwayne Conway behind bars. I'm a respected prosecuting attorney. Nobody will ever suspect me."

"What about Joel Asman? What does he have to do with this?"

"Nothing. I just paid that punk to stand outside on your sidewalk to freak you out."

"Chad, Dallas will be able to identify you. Somebody will know it was you," she replied desperately.

"Dallas didn't see who or what hit him, and my car is parked down the street. Nobody knows I'm here, Avery."

She screamed as his body slammed the door once

again. He was right. Nobody would suspect him. She certainly hadn't. Her stomach tightened once again, but she couldn't focus on that pain right now. She had to get the dresser in front of the door before he broke it down.

Lulu had disappeared under the bed. There was no such escape for Avery. She pushed with all her force on the dresser, sobbing and gasping for breath. Slowly it inched toward the door.

"I'm going to kill you, Avery, and I'm going to cut those babies out of your belly and kill them, too. That's what whores deserve."

"Is this what Danny wants?" she asked, trying to keep him talking. At least when he was talking he wasn't slamming into the door.

"Danny doesn't know anything about this and he'll never know. But if you continue to live it will torture him every day that he sees you happy with another man. If you're dead he can mourn you hard one time and then get on with his life. You have to die, Avery," Chad roared, and then slammed into the door with enough force that the sound of splintering wood filled the air.

With another scream and all the strength she had, she gave a final push on the dresser and it slid into place in front of the door.

Avery collapsed to the floor in front of the large piece of furniture, sobbing and struggling to catch her breath. She couldn't believe this was happening.

Chad had to be crazy. Apparently he'd been driven mad by his wife divorcing him.

He slammed into the door several more times, but couldn't get it to open with the weight of the dresser in front of it. Then everything went silent except for the sound of her own sobbing.

She managed to struggle to her feet, again ignoring the sharp pain that shot through her belly and back. Where was Chad? Was he just outside the bedroom door, waiting for her to venture out?

She didn't trust that the silence meant he was gone. She could identify him. She could tell everyone what he had done. There was no way he was just going to walk away from this situation now. Things had gone too far.

Within the silence of the house, one name screamed in her head over and over again. *Dallas. Dallas.* Even if she survived this night, would she have to live the rest of her life without Dallas in it? Would her babies not have their father?

Oh God, the thought of that filled her with an agony she'd never felt before. Her twins needed Dallas in their lives. She needed him. One way or another she had to have him in her life.

"Chad?" she called out. She needed to identify where he might be in the house. "Chad, talk to me. Please, Chad, can't we talk this out?"

The silence continued. It wasn't a peaceful silence, rather it was taut with the anticipation of an imminent explosion. She just didn't know exactly when it might take place or what might be destroyed.

Frantically, she gazed around the room, seeking something…anything that might be used as a weapon. In the bathroom all she found was a pair of manicure scissors, hardly any use against the big knife Chad had.

Still, she had a can of hair spray that could be aimed into his eyes and a bottle of rubbing alcohol that she could throw at him. They were meager weapons to use should he try to get into the room, but at least they were something.

She grabbed the hair spray from the bathroom vanity and then hurried back to the bedroom door. If he managed to get his face inside, she hoped she would blind him with the spray.

Her entire body was hurting, especially a pain that shot through her back. She must have pulled something while shoving the heavy dresser in front of the door. She ignored the pain. She had to stay alert and ready.

"Chad?" she yelled again. Her nerves were so taut she felt as if her body might fly into a million pieces at any moment. If he really wanted to, he probably could push his way through the door despite the dresser being there. He was a big man and enjoyed working out at the gym.

So where was he? What was he doing? Did he intend to keep her a prisoner in the bedroom until she broke? Until she starved to death?

Surely when morning came he'd be missing from work, or somebody would call to check on her. Maybe Breanna would phone, and when she couldn't reach Avery she'd come over to check on her. Somebody would recognize Chad's car parked down the street. No, he wouldn't want to be here in the morning.

Whatever was going to happen was going to do so fairly soon. Again her stomach tightened and pain rolled through her, pain intense enough that it nearly dropped her to her knees.

Then she realized what was happening. She was in labor. Heaven help her, it was too early. Her babies weren't supposed to come yet! She sat on the edge of the bed and tried to take deep, even breaths.

She needed to stop this from happening. She couldn't deliver the babies now, in a room where a man was waiting just outside to kill both her and them.

Fighting back hysterical sobs of hopelessness, she prayed for the labor pains to go away, for them to somehow be false pains brought on by the tremendous stress she was under.

"Chad, please talk to me," she yelled through the door. "It was never my intention to hurt Danny. I'll talk to him and make things right with him. We can just forget about all this and get back to our regular lives."

A shattering crash sounded behind her and she whirled around to see Chad coming in the bedroom window. She hadn't even thought about the window. With the pain racking her body she obviously hadn't been thinking clearly.

Before she could react, he was in the room. With the dresser in front of the door there was nowhere she could run. Even her bathroom was now too far away for her to reach.

"Chad...please," she said.

The man she'd believed a coworker, a teammate and a friend smiled at her, but it was like no smile she'd ever seen from him before. This one was filled with malice, with such hatred it stole her breath away.

"Danny's life would have been a happy one with you as his wife and him helping you raise your kids. But he wasn't good enough for you. The first chance you got you dumped him for one of the golden Coltons."

"Chad, you know it wasn't like that between me and Danny," she protested.

"But it could have been...it should have been," he screamed. He raised the knife and advanced toward her.

She raised the can of hair spray and pushed the button. The spray hit him in the eyes and he screamed once again as he raised his hands to his face.

She took the opportunity to run for the bathroom, but before she could get there he managed to grab her by the ankle and she tumbled to the floor.

Frantically, she kicked at him. Over and over again she kicked and thrashed in an effort to avoid the knife and escape his grasp.

She kicked him in the face and once again he yelled with his rage. "This is it, Avery. You're going to die."

A masculine roar sounded and Dallas came sailing through the window. He grabbed Chad by his shirt and yanked him up and off Avery. With a breathless gasp she scooted away and watched in horror as Dallas tried to kick the knife out of Chad's hand.

Dallas looked half-dead. Blood stained his forehead and shone through his hair. His face looked bloodless, but his eyes burned like piercing orbs as he faced off against Chad.

"Put the knife down, Chad," he said.

"She needs to die," the man replied. "Don't you see? Dallas, she's just going to use you. You'll be stuck raising those brats for years and then she'll dump you and move on. She's nothing but a whore."

Dallas leaped forward and slammed his fist into Chad's jaw, the blow throwing Chad backward. He recovered quickly and raised the knife over his head. With what sounded like a battle cry he attacked.

Avery screamed. Dallas managed to grab Chad's wrist and keep the knife away from him, but it was a battle of strength and Dallas appeared to be losing.

The knife got closer and closer to him. Strain showed on his face. "Dallas!" She screamed his name as another pain racked her body.

Her voice seemed to send a new burst of energy through him. With an enraged roar he managed to grab the knife from Chad. He tossed it over to Avery and then pulled his gun from the back of his jeans.

"It's over, Chad," he said wearily. "You should have frisked me when you knocked me out. I don't want to shoot you, but make no mistake that if necessary I will. Avery, go call Chief Thompson."

She got up from the floor. Dallas held Chad at gunpoint even as he shoved the dresser aside enough that she could leave the room. She managed to make it into the living room, where she pulled her phone from her purse. She made the call and then curled up in a ball on the floor as another agonizing pain felt like it was attempting to rip her in two.

She panted. It was over. Thank God, it was over. Chad would be arrested and she wouldn't have to worry about him for a long time to come.

What she worried about now was getting to the hospital. Her babies were coming whether she liked it or not. And they were early. And she was scared.

She was still on the floor in the living room when Chief Thompson and his men arrived. They came through the front door, which she hadn't locked after Chad's arrival.

Within minutes Dallas came into the living room, just as another pain swept over her. She released a deep moan.

"Avery. Honey, are you hurt?" Dallas crouched down next to her. "Did he hurt you?"

For a moment she couldn't reply. She did manage to grab Dallas's hand as she panted to catch her breath. "No...no, he didn't hurt me," she gasped when she could. "The babies are coming." She squeezed his hand more tightly. "Dallas, the babies are coming and I'm so scared."

Chapter 14

Thankfully, an ambulance had responded to the scene at Avery's house. Dallas scooped her up in his arms and carried her outside to the vehicle, where she was placed on the gurney.

"Go, go, go!" he yelled at the driver, as he crawled into the back with Avery and the paramedic.

The ambulance took off and a cry from Avery rivaled the siren overhead. "Do something," he said frantically to the paramedic. "She's in pain."

The young man gave Dallas a patient smile. "She's in labor, sir. I've already contacted the hospital and they know we're on our way."

At least the man took Avery's vitals, but before he was finished she was writhing and moaning once again. "Avery, honey." Dallas pushed a strand of hair away from her face. "I'm sorry. I'm so sorry."

Her eyes focused on him for a moment and she released a burst of laughter. "What are you sorry for? You aren't the one being rendered apart by children fighting over who gets to be the oldest."

"But if I could take this pain away from you, I would. Honest to God, Avery, I'd take the pain from you."

She slapped him lightly on the arm. "Oh, shut up, man, and leave the hard stuff to us women of the world. This is why only women give birth...because men can't handle it."

"Are we almost there?" Dallas called to the driver as Avery moaned deep in the back of her throat. It was a moan of such pain that tears sprang to his eyes.

Was this the way it was supposed to be or was she in some kind of danger because the twins were coming two and a half weeks early? Was something wrong?

His head throbbed and he felt slightly nauseous, but he couldn't think about that right now. Finally, they reached the hospital, where emergency staff were waiting to whisk her away.

"If you're planning on seeing the births of your babies, then you better have a doctor look at that head wound and let me clean it up for you," Sandra Bowen said. She was a nurse and a friendly acquaintance of his.

He looked at her frantically. "I don't have time for that. I need to get in there to be with her right now. The babies are coming."

"We were told her pains were about three to four minutes apart. We have time to clean up your head before they arrive. Besides, you want to be looking your best when they get their first look at you. Right now you'd probably scare them with all that blood on your face."

He relented and went with her to an examining room, where she cleaned up the blood and an X-ray was taken. One of the doctors came in to tell him he had a mild concussion, but even if his skull was cracked in a hundred pieces, all he wanted was to be with Avery.

Finally, he was escorted into the room where she was in bed with her feet in stirrups and a soft blanket covering her. A nurse was standing by her head, where a monitor beeped and an IV bag was hooked up.

"Avery!" He rushed to her side. "How are you doing?"

She smiled at him, and she'd never looked so beautiful to him. "I'm doing *fine*…!" She rolled her head back and forth on the pillow as another pain struck her.

"How long does this last?" Dallas asked the nurse.

She laughed. "Who knows? Babies come in their own time. It could just be an hour or two or it could be morning before they arrive."

"Morning?" he gasped. "Can you give her something for the pain?"

"Dallas, I'm fine," Avery said. "This is normal and I can't have anything for the pain. This is what birth is all about, and I can't wait to hold these babies in my arms."

For the next three hours Avery suffered with the labor pains. Dallas sat next to her and held her hand and helped her breathe through the contractions.

During that time Dr. Sanders came into the room several times to check on her patient. Dallas looked up as she came into the room once more. "How are we doing?" she asked brightly.

"I'm never having sex again," Avery said with a gasp.

Dr. Sanders laughed. "I've heard that sentiment a time or two before, but usually within a year or two the women are back in here to give birth to their second or third child. Now, let's do a check and see where we're at."

Avery panted, as if she couldn't draw enough oxygen. Her eyes suddenly held a look of wild panic that scared the hell out of Dallas.

The doctor checked several things and then frowned. "I think we have an issue." She turned to the nurse in the room. "We need to go ahead and get her into the operating room for a C-section. Both the babies and Avery are in distress."

Before Dallas could wrap his mind around what

was happening, Avery was gone and he was in the waiting room. An agonizing fear filled him. Both Avery and the babies were in distress? So much so that they'd wheeled her into an operating room?

What was happening? Had he saved Avery from Chad only to lose her to childbirth? He didn't want to lose his babies. He also didn't want to lose Avery. Dr. Sanders had to save them all.

He paced the waiting room and thought about everything that had happened from the moment he had seen Avery on the top of the courthouse steps. She had looked so beautiful, and instantly his heart had beat a little faster as he'd remembered the night they had spent together.

His mind created a reel of moments they had spent together since the day she'd come into his life. They had shared so much laughter. There had been so many nights of contentment with her.

Finally, he thought about what she had said to him right before the rock sailed through her window. She had told him she was in love with him and that she wanted to spend all her days and nights with him.

With everything that had happened, he'd scarcely had time to take in what she'd told him. And now he could only pray that she would survive the birth so he could tell her what he wanted for the future.

Avery came to consciousness slowly. For several moments she was confused and disoriented. The first thing she noticed was the sun peeking up over the horizon at the nearby window. She frowned. Where had the night gone? She frowned again as she realized she was in a hospital bed and an IV was connected to her arm.

She turned her head to see Dallas slumped down in a chair. He was sound asleep, with lines of exhaustion etched into his forehead.

As the fog that had encased her brain slowly lifted, she remembered the night. Chad trying to kill her...the labor pains...her babies! Her hands flew to her relatively flat stomach. She didn't remember giving birth. Why didn't she remember? Oh God, what had happened to her babies?

"Dallas," she said, but her voice was a mere dry whisper. She cleared her throat and tried again, frantic to find out what had happened. "Dallas."

His eyes shot open and he jumped up out of his chair and rushed to her side. "Avery, honey...thank God you're awake. Thank God you're okay. How are you feeling?"

"The babies...what happened to the babies?" she asked, panicked now that she was fully conscious and couldn't remember what exactly had happened.

"They're fine." Dallas's wide smile shot a shudder of relief through her. "They're beautiful, Avery. They're a bit small, but they are both absolutely perfect. Our son arrived two minutes before his little sister."

"I need to see them. I need to hold them," she said.

"First, let me go get the doctor. I'll let her know you're awake," he said. He reached the door and turned back to look at her. "Avery, you scared the hell out of me last night. I thought… I thought I was going to lose you…lose everything." He then disappeared out the door.

Avery released a tremulous sigh. He must have been worried about the babies. That's what he meant when he'd said he'd been afraid he'd lose everything.

Now that she was more fully awake, she had a bit of pain in her stomach. She realized she'd had a C-section. She looked out the window once again.

Dawn light promised a new day…a wonderful day. She'd given birth to two perfect babies. Joy filled her, a tremendous joy she'd never felt before. She felt as if nobody had ever given birth before her, that she had created a miracle that the world had never seen before.

Nothing that had happened before this moment mattered to her. She just wanted to hold her son and her daughter. She wanted to smell their newborn sweet innocence and revel in their very presence.

Dallas came back into the room with Dr. Sanders. "How is our new mom?" Dr. Sanders asked.

"I'm okay. My stomach hurts a bit, but all I want is my babies in my arms," Avery replied.

"Let me just get a peek at your staples and then we'll bring them in." Dr. Sanders checked her abdomen. "You're looking good, Mama. You gave us all a little scare, but thankfully all is well that ends well."

"I just want my babies," Avery replied. She winced as she changed position.

"We'll bring you the babies and I'll have the nurse give you a little pain medicine," Dr. Sanders said.

At that moment a nurse walked in carrying a baby in each arm. Happy tears sprang to Avery's eyes. She didn't care about pain medicine; all she wanted was those babies in her arms. The nurse handed her first her son and then her daughter.

They were both asleep, but she cuddled them close against her. They were not only perfect, they were absolutely beautiful. Little tufts of golden hair covered their heads and their little features were absolute perfection. Dallas stood next to her, his gaze focused on her and his children.

"We'll just leave you alone," Dr. Sanders said, and motioned for the nurse to follow her out of the room.

"I've never known this kind of love before," Avery said softly as she gazed down at the newborns.

"I know exactly what you mean," Dallas said. "I told you they were perfect."

"They are so beautiful they almost take my breath away."

The nurse came back in with a syringe in her hand. "This will help take the edge off your pain," she said as she administered the drug into the IV.

"The best pain med is holding these babies," Avery replied.

"They are sweethearts." The woman smiled as she left the room.

At that moment Danny appeared in the doorway. He held a vase full of flowers and he appeared positively tortured. "I... Could I come in for just a minute? I'll understand if you don't want to see or talk to me." He appeared to be on the verge of tears.

Avery looked at Dallas and then back at him. "Come in, Danny."

He took two steps into the room. Dallas took the flowers from him and carried them to a nearby table. "First of all, congratulations." Danny's voice trembled with emotion. "I'm so glad you're all okay."

"Thank you. We're very happy," Dallas replied.

"I didn't know." The words seemed to be ripped from the back of Danny's throat. "I swear I didn't know about Chad trying to hurt you." Tears sprang to Danny's eyes. "If I had known I would have stopped him."

He looked at Avery and then at Dallas. "I couldn't believe it when I heard what had happened, what he did, and that he told you he was doing it for me. I can't even wrap my head around how sick he is."

Tears fell down his cheeks and again he looked like a man undergoing torture. "I just want you to be happy, Avery." He looked at Dallas. "And I know you make her happy. I just needed you both to know that I had nothing to do with the madness that happened last night."

"I know that, Danny." Avery smiled at him. She

didn't blame him for Chad's actions. Danny had been as much an innocent victim as she had been.

"I'm so sorry. I'm so damned sorry," Danny choked out.

Dallas walked over to him and held out his hand for a shake. "We're good, man."

Danny hesitated and then grabbed Dallas's hand. The two men shook and then Danny took a step backward. "I'll just get out of here now and leave you alone."

"Thanks for the flowers," Avery said.

"It was the very least I could do," he replied, and then he turned and left the room.

"I think Chad's actions are going to haunt Danny for a long time to come," Avery said.

"I think you're right. Hopefully, he doesn't beat himself up for too long," Dallas replied, and then moved closer to the side of the bed. "And now I think we have some unfinished business between us."

"Unfinished business?" She looked at him in bewilderment.

"Before that rock sailed through your window and things got crazy, you told me something."

She suddenly remembered her confession of love. It seemed like a lifetime ago that she'd told him how much she loved him and wanted him in her life, not just as a coparent, but as a forever kind of man.

Now she was embarrassed by her outburst, and she certainly didn't want this first moment with her babies to be tainted by him telling her he didn't love her that way.

"It's okay, Dallas. Let's just celebrate our twins. Have you gotten to hold them yet?"

"I have. They are little miracles. But they do need names."

She relaxed. "Yes, it's time to get serious about their names." She leaned down and first kissed her son's forehead and then her daughter's. Her heart once again swelled with immense joy. "Actually, I'd like to call our son Ezekiel Dallas Colton, if you'd be okay with that." She looked at Dallas cautiously.

He smiled. "I think that's a fine name for our son. What about our little girl?"

"If you want to name her Ivy, I wouldn't have a problem with that," she replied.

Dallas took a step closer. "Avery, while I appreciate that, Ivy is a part of my past. Actually, what do you think about Ariana Josephine?"

"That's beautiful," Avery replied. "Ezekiel and Ariana. I think we have winners."

"And now we need to talk about us. Is it really true, what you told me last night before everything went crazy?" His gaze bored into hers. "Did you mean it when you said you love me and you want to spend all your days and nights with me?"

She was afraid to tell him again what was in her heart. She was terrified he would reject her and then things would get awkward. The babies were here now and the last thing she wanted was any tension or awkwardness between her and Dallas.

"I meant every word I said, but we can forget all that now and just enjoy our lives as coparents to these sweet babies."

"I don't want to forget it," he replied. "After you told me how you felt about me, I didn't get an opportunity to tell you how I felt…how I feel about you."

Avery's heart trembled with anxiety as she stared at the man she loved. At the moment his features were unreadable. She couldn't begin to guess what he was about to say.

He leaned toward her, so close she could smell the familiar scent of him, a scent that had come to represent love and safety to her.

"When I lost Ivy, I swore I would never love another woman. I'd had my shot at loving and fate had cruelly snatched that away. But then that same fate brought me you, and with the promise of the twins I realized I could be happy again."

"I'm glad, Dallas. I want you to be happy," she replied.

"But just being happy as a single father isn't enough for me, Avery. I want it all. I want you and the twins in my life all day and all night for the rest of my life." His blue eyes suddenly shone with a light that washed a wave of welcomed heat through her.

"I love you, Avery. I love you with all my heart and soul."

She wanted to believe him. She wanted to believe him so badly, but she was afraid. "Dallas, please don't love me because of the twins," she said in a soft whisper.

"Avery, don't short-change yourself. There's nothing I want more in my life than a fierce woman who puts away bad guys, loves her children and loves me to distraction."

"Oh, Dallas, I am that woman, and I want to be that woman forever." Tears misted her vision.

"Then promise that you'll marry me. As soon as you get out of the hospital, as soon as we can make it happen, promise you'll marry me and make me the happiest man on earth," he said.

His love for her was unmistakable. It shone from his eyes and trembled in his deep voice. She laughed, the noise making both babies frown and then begin to cry.

"Yes," she said joyously, over the sound of their twins' lusty voices. "Yes, Dallas, I'll marry you."

He leaned down and captured her lips with his, and in the kiss she tasted love and commitment. She tasted a future filled with love and laughter and chaos. Oh yes, there would be chaos with the twins. But she knew they'd meet each challenge that came their way together, with united hearts and a love that would last them a lifetime.

* * * * *

Don't miss the exciting conclusion of
Colton 911 with the next story:
Colton 911: Deadly Texas Reunion
by Beth Cornelison,
available next month from
Harlequin Romantic Suspense.

For a sneak peek, turn the page.

Prologue

FBI Special Agent Nolan Colton hated suits almost as much as he hated today's unexpected summons to his boss's office. As he waited to be called back, he tugged at the collar of his dress shirt and readjusted the tie that threatened to strangle him. His knee bounced while he waited. Patience had never been his forte. What the hell could have happened to warrant this urgent confab with the special agent in charge? Nothing good. Nolan reached in his coat pocket for an antacid and chewed it. His gut had been torn up with dread all night. His boss's tone of voice when he'd called last night instructing Nolan to report to this meeting had been grave and terse.

When the SAC's administrative assistant finally called him to the inner office, he took a deep breath, tugged his shirtsleeves to straighten them and strode into his boss's domain with his head high and his back ramrod straight.

The first thing Nolan noticed when he entered Special Agent in Charge Dean Humboldt's office was they weren't alone. Deputy Assistant Director Jim Greenley sat in one of the chairs opposite Humboldt, and a man Nolan didn't know but who seemed vaguely familiar occupied the seat to the left of Humboldt's desk. The second thing Nolan noticed was he wasn't invited to take a seat.

He assumed a rigid stance, feet slightly apart, shoulders back, hands clasped behind him. "Good morning, sirs."

"Special Agent Colton," the deputy assistant director said by way of greeting, adding a quick dip of his chin.

The SAC's administrative assistant left, closing the door behind her, and Nolan felt a brief moment of claustrophobia. His tie seemed to tighten like a noose.

"Thank you for coming this morning, Special Agent Colton," Humboldt said.

"I didn't get the impression when you called me last night that I had a choice."

Humboldt cleared his throat. "No. A rather serious matter has been brought to my attention, and we need to address it."

"I've never known the Bureau to handle anything that wasn't serious." He twitched a grin, but his attempt at humor fell flat. Humboldt scowled, and Greenley exchanged a look with the third man, who had yet to be introduced. "Sorry. What matter is that, sir?"

Humboldt opened a manila file folder on his desk and slid a large black-and-white photograph across the desk. "This."

Nolan stepped forward to look at the picture, and what he saw there shot adrenaline to his marrow. A photo of himself. In an erotic and compromising position with a fellow special agent.

Well, hell. He'd thought the ill-advised, one-time tryst with his partner had been discreet, something he could bury. They'd been alone in her hotel room. So where had the picture come from? The obvious answer rattled him. Angered him.

"Um…" Nolan blinked. "Where did you get this?"

"We're asking the questions today, Special Agent Colton," Greenley said.

"You recognize the woman in the photo, Special Agent?"

He jerked a nod. "Special Agent Charlotte O'Toole. We worked a case together last year in Portland." He drew a slow breath, deciding honesty was his best policy. "Obviously, things got out of control one night. It was a mistake, but it was just a one-time thing."

Humboldt divided a glance between the other two men. Greenley arched one graying eyebrow.

When Humboldt slid another picture toward him with much the same content, Nolan gritted his back teeth.

"What is it you say happened that night, Special Agent Colton?" Humboldt asked. His boss's continued formal use of his official title rather than his first name unsettled Nolan.

He frowned and tilted his head in confusion. "I'd think that was pretty clear. Are you asking for scurrilous details? Because I have to say, sir, I find it crass of a man to kiss and tell."

Humboldt folded his hands on his desk. "Generally I do, too. But considering the allegations Special Agent O'Toole has made against you, I think you'd be wise to share your side of the events of that night."

A chill raced down Nolan's spine. "Allegations?" He could barely choke the word out. His pulse thundered in his ears as he looked from one grim face to another. "Wh-what is she alleging?"

"She claims you assaulted her."

Nolan's blood froze, and he had the very real, very scary sense of his career, his reputation, slipping away like a wild mustang jerking the reins from his hands. He struggled for a breath. "What?"

"Special Agent O'Toole came forward last week with claims that you made advances toward her over a period of several days while you two were on assignment. She claims she consistently rebuffed your advances and reminded you such behavior was both unprofessional and unwelcome by her."

Disbelief clogged Nolan's throat. He made sputtering noises, but shock rendered him mute.

"Believing she would need evidence of your behavior to substantiate her claim, she hid a camera to capture further incidents as proof."

More like she wanted to frame him. Nolan's hands fisted. He'd been set up. But *why?*

Humboldt tapped the file folder. "There are more if you'd like to see them, but they are much alike and tell the same story."

Nolan glanced at the incriminating picture again, noting this time that the shot showed him bowing Charlotte back, as if the aggressor, while her hands were against his chest as if pushing him away. Her head was turned as if avoiding his kiss instead of providing access to her slim neck and bared shoulder.

Fighting for composure, Nolan said gruffly, "I'd like to see the other pictures, just the same."

His boss handed him the file.

Beside Humboldt's desk, the third man huffed irritably, but Nolan ignored him as he thumbed through the rest of the snapshots. Every one of the images gave the impression that Nolan had been an assailant and Charlotte his unwilling victim. Which was far from the truth. Missing from the file were dozens of other moments in which Charlotte had seduced him, pressured him, ravaged him. He saw now that she'd made a point of staging plenty of poses providing evidence to the contrary. But still he wondered, why?

He and Charlotte had worked well together. He'd liked her—obviously—and thought they had a good professional and personal relationship. So what had made her turn on him? No. Not turn on him. That indicated a change of heart. For her to plant the camera, pose the pictures and pursue him with the fervor that she had—because she had, in fact, been the instigator, pushing him to violate his professional ethics for the one-night stand—this whole situation had been premeditated. Charlotte had used him. Betrayed him.

"That bitch," Nolan muttered under his breath.

The third man puffed up and growled, "I'll thank you not to speak that way about *my wife*."

Freshly stunned, Nolan jerked his gaze to the older man. "Your wife?"

"You didn't know?" Greenley asked.

Nolan snorted, no longer caring about comportment or respect for his superiors. "Obviously not."

He was being railroaded with false charges, and he would defend himself with everything he had.

Greenley turned up a palm. "Special Agent O'Toole married the senator five years ago."

"Six years ago," the third man corrected.

Nolan gave his head a small shake as if he'd heard wrong. "I'm sorry...the *senator*?"

Humboldt nodded toward the man in question. "Yes. US Senator George Dell of Nebraska."

Holy crap. He'd slept with the wife of a US senator? And Charlotte had said nothing about a husband, and certainly not a husband with so much power.

The bad vibe he'd had even before entering Humboldt's office had cranked up by a factor of ten. A hundred.

Nolan's entire body tensed. Fire flashed through his veins. He thought his heart might pound right through his chest. A kaleidoscope of emotions battled for dominance as his brain numbly processed the accusation and ramifications. He had to lock his knees to keep his shaking legs under him. "Th-this is all, uh...a big misunderstanding."

"You're denying her claims?" Humboldt asked.

He jerked a stunned gaze to his boss. Humboldt had worked with him long enough to know Nolan's character better than that. How could his boss even *think* he was capable of such a heinous thing?

He threw the folder of photos back on Humboldt's desk. "Hell, yes, I deny it! I'm not a sexual assailant!"

The senator shoved to his feet, his hands balled. "So you're calling my wife a liar?"

Nolan reeled in the curt reply on his tongue at the last possible moment. He needed to be careful what he said, how he said it. He didn't want his accusers to have any more rope to hang him with. As it was, defending himself from charges of sexual assault would be tricky at best.

He struggled for a calm tone as he faced the senator, but a throbbing pulse pounded at his temples. "All I can tell you is that I didn't know Charlotte was married, and what happened between us was *not* assault. I know you don't want to hear it, but it was one hundred percent consensual."

Nolan stood his ground as the senator took two aggressive steps toward him, his teeth gritted and bared, his face florid. "You son of a—"

Greenley caught the senator's arm. "Sir, please. Have a seat."

Turning back to Humboldt, Nolan scrubbed a hand down his face. "Sir, you *know* me. You know these charges are preposterous. I would never...could *never*..."

"My personal opinion doesn't matter." Humboldt's expression was stern but apologetic. "A matter of this magnitude requires an internal investigation."

An investigation. Somehow knowing the incident would be explored gave Nolan a seed of hope. Surely the investigation would uncover the truth. He'd be exonerated and his name cleared, his reputation—

"Until the investigation is complete, you're hereby suspended without pay—"

"What?" he shouted, gut-punched.

"Effective immediately." Humboldt stuck his hand out. "I need your badge and your service weapon."

Nolan gaped at his boss. This *couldn't* be happening. His career was *everything* to him. This smear to his character and reputation, even if he was found innocent, would follow him forever.

He cut a glance to Greenley, praying for reprieve, but met a stony countenance.

"I swear I didn't… I'd never…" He shook his head, and his chest contracted so hard he couldn't catch his breath.

Humboldt's hand was still extended to him, but Nolan refused to let the senator, whose smug grin gnawed at Nolan, see him surrender his weapon.

"This is bullshit!" Nolan turned on his heel and marched out of the office.

He'd made it as far as the elevator when Humboldt caught up to him. "Nolan, wait!"

Whirling around, he jabbed a finger toward his boss—ex-boss?—and growled, "You *know* I didn't do what she's accusing me of. I would *never* take advantage of a woman that way! Hell, man, you trusted me to drive your daughter to her apartment after the barbecue back in July!"

"I have no choice," Humboldt said, holding out his hand, palm up, again. "Damn it, Nolan. My hands are tied. It's your word against hers, and she has incriminating photographs."

Seething, Nolan unfastened his holster and slapped his service weapon into his boss's hand. "Yeah, well-selected photos. But where are the ones of the times in between the posed shots? She was all over me, Dean. It was her idea, and she took the lead, no matter what the pictures say."

"Your badge and ID."

Nolan groaned in frustration as he fished in his pocket for his credentials. "We've had this discussion before—how much we both abhor the sort of man who harasses and demeans women. God, it makes me *sick* to be lumped in the same category with scum like that!" He smacked his FBI shield and ID wallet into Humboldt's hand. "I have no idea what's behind all this. But, please, Dean, don't let them railroad me. This has to be political or… I don't know. But it's a load of crap. I swear!"

To his credit, Humboldt looked grief stricken as he shook his head. "Go home, Nolan. Use the time to…go fishing or see old friends."

He scoffed. "Fishing? That's all you have for me?"

His boss lifted a shoulder. "I'm sorry."

Nolan jabbed the elevator button before deciding to take the stairs. He had adrenaline to burn off. Stalking away, he fisted his hands at his sides. The injustice clawed at him. After so many years working to get where he was within the Bureau, it had been

snatched away in a heartbeat. And the best his boss
had was "Go fishing or see old friends"?

As he slammed through the stairwell door and
descended the steps two at a time, an image came
to him, fixed itself in his head. And he knew where
he'd go until this nightmare was resolved.

Whisperwood.

Get 4 FREE REWARDS!

We'll send you 2 FREE Books plus 2 FREE Mystery Gifts.

Harlequin® Romantic Suspense books feature heart-racing sensuality and the promise of a sweeping romance set against the backdrop of suspense.

FREE
Value Over **$20**

YES! Please send me 2 FREE Harlequin® Romantic Suspense novels and my 2 FREE gifts (gifts are worth about $10 retail). After receiving them, if I don't wish to receive any more books, I can return the shipping statement marked "cancel." If I don't cancel, I will receive 4 brand-new novels every month and be billed just $4.99 per book in the U.S. or $5.74 per book in Canada. That's a savings of at least 12% off the cover price! It's quite a bargain! Shipping and handling is just 50¢ per book in the U.S. and $1.25 per book in Canada.* I understand that accepting the 2 free books and gifts places me under no obligation to buy anything. I can always return a shipment and cancel at any time. The free books and gifts are mine to keep no matter what I decide.

240/340 HDN GNMZ

Name (please print)

Address   Apt. #

City   State/Province   Zip/Postal Code

Mail to the **Reader Service:**
IN U.S.A.: P.O. Box 1341, Buffalo, NY 14240-8531
IN CANADA: P.O. Box 603, Fort Erie, Ontario L2A 5X3

Want to try 2 free books from another series? Call 1-800-873-8635 or visit www.ReaderService.com.

---

*Terms and prices subject to change without notice. Prices do not include sales taxes, which will be charged (if applicable) based on your state or country of residence. Canadian residents will be charged applicable taxes. Offer not valid in Quebec. This offer is limited to one order per household. Books received may not be as shown. Not valid for current subscribers to Harlequin® Romantic Suspense books. All orders subject to approval. Credit or debit balances in a customer's account(s) may be offset by any other outstanding balance owed by or to the customer. Please allow 4 to 6 weeks for delivery. Offer available while quantities last.

Your Privacy—The Reader Service is committed to protecting your privacy. Our Privacy Policy is available online at www.ReaderService.com or upon request from the Reader Service. We make a portion of our mailing list available to reputable third parties that offer products we believe may interest you. If you prefer that we not exchange your name with third parties, or if you wish to clarify or modify your communication preferences, please visit us at www.ReaderService.com/consumerschoice or write to us at Reader Service Preference Service, P.O. Box 9062, Buffalo, NY 14240-9062. Include your complete name and address.

HRS19R3

"I appreciate you coming," he said.

"You said it was important."

Paul nodded as he gestured for her to take a seat.
Sitting down, Simone stole another quick glance toward
the bar. The two strangers were both staring blatantly, not
bothering to hide their interest in the two of them.

Simone rested an elbow on the tabletop, turning
flirtatiously toward her friend. "Do you know Tom and
Jerry over there at the bar?" she asked softly. She reached
a hand out, trailing her fingers against his arm.

Her touch was just distracting enough that Paul didn't
turn abruptly to stare back, drawing even more attention
in their direction. His focus shifted slowly from her
toward the duo at the bar. He eyed them briefly before

turning his attention back to Simone. He shook his head. "Should I?"

"It might be nothing, but they seem very interested in you."

Paul's gaze danced back in their direction and he took a swift inhale of air. One of the men was on a cell phone and both were still eyeing him intently.

"We need to leave," he said, suddenly anxious. He began to gather his papers.

"What's going on, Paul?"

"I don't think we're safe, Simone."

"What do you mean we're not safe?" she snapped, her teeth clenched tightly. "Why are we not safe?"

"I'll explain, but I think we really need to leave."

Simone took a deep breath and held it, watching as he repacked his belongings into his briefcase.

"We're not going anywhere until you explain," she started, and then a commotion at the door pulled at her attention.

Don't miss
Reunited by the Badge *by Deborah Fletcher Mello*
available October 2019 wherever
Harlequin® *Romantic Suspense*
books and ebooks are sold.

www.Harlequin.com

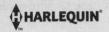

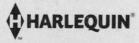

Love Harlequin romance?

DISCOVER.

Be the first to find out about promotions, news and exclusive content!

Facebook.com/HarlequinBooks

Twitter.com/HarlequinBooks

Instagram.com/HarlequinBooks

Pinterest.com/HarlequinBooks

ReaderService.com

EXPLORE.

Sign up for the Harlequin e-newsletter and download a free book from any series at **TryHarlequin.com.**

CONNECT.

Join our Harlequin community to share your thoughts and connect with other romance readers!
Facebook.com/groups/HarlequinConnection

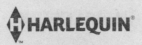

**ROMANCE WHEN
YOU NEED IT**

HSOCIAL2018